LOVE IN THE ROCKIES

TRUE LOVE TRAVELS BOOK ONE

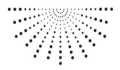

POPPY PENNINGTON-SMITH

TRUE LOVE TRAVELS

CHAPTER ONE

*B*eth Greenwood shrugged herself into the too big sweater her grandmother knitted last Christmas, filled a mug with strong dark coffee, and took the large silver key from its hook in the hall. She didn't bother to comb her hair and, despite the frost covering the ground outside, she remained barefoot.

There were fifteen steps from her back door to the garden shed she used as a writing room. Each one made her toes tingle, but as soon as she was inside she wriggled them into her fleece-lined slipper socks and jigged up and down.

Her father's old chair was in the corner nearest the electric heater, but in the three years since he died she hadn't dared to move it. So, she sat opposite and waited for the warmth to reach her.

Her father had never used a desk, or a computer, to write. He'd sat in his bottle-green, high-backed chair with a tray

1

and a typewriter on his lap. Beth had tried to do the same, but her lap was too small and the typewriter too big. So, now, it perched precariously on a small fold-out table that wobbled whenever she punched the letter 'B'.

She glanced at the clock. Six a.m. One hour's writing time before the people of Oxford started to wake and she was expected at the office. She should probably be using the time to do yoga or curl her hair, but this time of the morning was her favourite part of the day.

Her father had been a night-owl. He'd preferred to tuck himself away and write while the world drank wine in pubs or binge-watched Netflix. Her boyfriend Harry was the same – always texting at absurd times of the night when he was up late working. But Beth liked mornings. Even if she only managed a few words, it made her feel like she'd snatched some time that the rest of the world had been too busy sleeping to enjoy.

Today, she was supposed to be writing a blog post about backpacks. The best backpacks to take on a European city break. Soul-suckingly boring, but the kind of quick, easy-to-read content that people craved. A *listicle* they called it – a cross between an article and a list. But she just couldn't bring herself to do it; she knew she should be writing material that would generate traffic for her site – that getting visitor numbers up was the only way she'd start making money – but, mostly, whenever she tried to write to a template or a style that was popular, she ended up going off-piste and writing something entirely different.

On the shelf behind her, wedged next to a well-thumbed copy of *The Great Railway Bazaar*, was the iPad Harry had bought her. Nearly every time he saw her, he tutted and said that it was utterly ridiculous of her to write her posts on the typewriter and then go through the 'rigmarole' of typing them up on her laptop. But Beth found it almost impossible to think without the clunk-clunk of the keys. And so, to prove him wrong, she'd successfully ignored the iPad for almost two whole months.

Her father would never have used an iPad to write; he was a different kind of writer – a *real* travel writer. He'd written travel guides, magazine articles, and just before he died he'd started work on his seventh book.

Beth sighed and sipped her coffee. Every inch of wall inside the shed was covered with postcards, newspaper clippings, and photographs celebrating her father's illustrious career. And every time she looked at them, she felt disappointed in herself.

He had always told her to follow her dreams. He'd told her that when she turned eighteen they would go on an incredible journey that would fill her head with wonder and inspiration, and then maybe they'd write a book together, persuade Mum to travel with them. His favourite place in the world was Canada – it was the first place he went when he started writing for magazines, and he'd always longed to take her mother to Niagara Falls.

But then he'd gotten sick.

Their magical trip never happened. And now Beth was

twenty-nine years old and still working as a non-travelling travel agent with Cooper's – a small, independent firm that specialised in exotic honeymoons but hadn't managed to spread its wings much further than Oxfordshire.

Cooper's was where she'd met Harry. Dependable, type-writer-hating Harry. Harry with his coordinated suits, perfect hair, and clear-cut path to upper management. Harry who had absolutely no desire to travel and every desire for Beth to settle down and accept that writing for fun was fine but writing in the hope of building a career would lead to nothing but disappointment.

In the beginning, their differences hadn't seemed to matter very much. Beth had been so wrapped up in her father's illness and Harry had been charming and easy and so good at taking charge. He'd driven her to the hospital, distracted her with romantic home-cooked meals, stood by her side at the funeral, let her yell and cry and spend all day eating chocolate on the couch.

But now the mist was clearing, she found him... irritating. And she knew that was awful of her.

Every day, she began with the resolution to 'snap out of it' and start warming to him again. But every day, she went to bed with a niggling feeling deep in her stomach that told her things were not going well between them. It wasn't helped by the fact that Harry had started dropping hints about them moving in together. So far, Beth had managed to avoid giving him a direct answer. But it wouldn't be long before he asked her outright and she had to decide one way or the other.

Glancing at the notes on her phone, she forced herself to stop thinking about her Harry-conundrum and start typing. And by the time her alarm sounded at six fifty-five, she'd managed five-hundred words of the backpack article.

Leaving her empty cup on the desk, she locked the shed behind her and tip-toed back inside.

"Morning love, coffee?"

Beth glanced guiltily back at the shed. She'd developed a nasty habit of drinking two coffees before she even left the house and kept telling herself she'd switch to decaf. "Yes, thanks." She kissed her mum on the cheek and leaned back on the kitchen table, fiddling absentmindedly with the pendant that hung around her neck. It was a birthstone that her father had given her and she barely ever took it off.

"How's it going?" Mum gestured to Beth's article.

Beth sighed. "Slowly."

"These things take time. Your father spent years earning barely a penny before he became successful."

"I know."

Mum handed her a plate of toast and squeezed her arm. "He'd be proud of you. You'll get there."

Beth smiled, but it turned into more of a grimace.

"What is it, Beth?"

"It's just… I'm not getting there, am I?"

"Of course you are. You're doing really well."

"But I'm not though." She laughed, even though it wasn't funny, and tossed her fly-away hair over her shoulder. "I'm a travel blogger working for a travel agency and I don't have the time to actually travel! It's kind of ridiculous. And until I do, everything I write will just be hollow. Dredged up. Soulless."

Mum rolled her eyes and tutted. "That's a little dramatic, don't you think?"

"No," Beth replied defensively. She bit off a chunk of toast and shook her head. "The thing is, I look at what other people are doing and I just think there's no way I'll ever be able to compete."

"Other people?"

"Other travel bloggers. Like..." Beth reached for her phone, navigated quickly to Instagram and waved it beneath her mother's nose. "This guy. Blake O'Brien. He's Canadian and he built his blog from nothing in under a year. He's got an enormous following. He's travelling all over the world. And he's actually making money."

Mum squinted at the phone. "He's very good looking."

"That's not really the point–"

"Well, listen honey, there's no reason you can't do exactly what he's done. You're very talented."

Beth ignored the compliment and put down her toast so she could wave her arms. "Blake publishes something every single day. He's all over social media. The only way I'd be able to do that is if I quit working at Cooper's."

Her mother leaned back against the worktop and softened her expression. "Beth, your father left you that money. If you need to stop work to make your dreams happen, he'd support that. You can use the money to–"

"No. I'm not using it for that."

Mum bit her lip to disguise a sigh. She was speaking gently, as if Beth was still a teenager resisting good advice. "So, then take some time off. Take a vacation. Go somewhere exciting, get your mojo back, use the time to get a head start on writing some more material."

"I can't. I took four days peak-season for Harry's silly friends and their silly middle-of-nowhere wedding, so I daren't take any more. Besides, you'd be on your own…"

"I'm a grownup, Beth."

"But you haven't been alone since Dad…" she trailed off and looked down at her fingernails.

Accepting defeat, Mum glanced at the clock. "Shouldn't you be getting dressed? Harry will be here soon."

She was right; Harry picked Beth up at seven forty every morning. For a moment, Beth wondered whether she could eat her toast on the way. But Harry hated crumbs. He'd have a fit if she got toast dust all over the passenger seat. So, she tucked her article into the kitchen drawer and scurried upstairs to get ready for yet another scintillating day being a sensible person with a sensible job.

An hour later, stomach rumbling, Beth unbuckled her seatbelt as Harry manoeuvred his shiny new Audi into its usual parking space. Planting his hand firmly on her upper thigh,

Harry leaned in and kissed her neck. "Why do you always smell so lovely?"

"Because I shower," Beth replied, shrugging out of his grasp and narrowing her eyes at her phone.

"What are you so engrossed in?" Harry squeezed a little closer and peered over her shoulder.

"I'm just..." Beth paused. Her stomach tightened.

"What is it?"

Beth's lips stretched into a grin. She shook her head, then waved the phone at Harry. "Blake O'Brien just recommended one of my articles on his blog."

Harry's brow crinkled. "Blake O'Who?"

"I've got two-hundred new followers!"

Harry patted Beth's leg and smiled at her. "Is this guy a big deal?"

"Just a bit!" Beth passed her phone to Harry. "Look. He has thousands of followers. He's making a fortune with his blog. He's pretty much an inspiration. I mean, he only started out a year ago and–"

Harry glanced at the screen, then passed it quickly back. "Beth," he said. "Obviously, this guy is doing great things. But we've talked about this, haven't we?"

"Hmm?" Beth was so engrossed in reading the comments Blake's followers had left on her post that she was barely taking in what Harry was saying.

"Some people are lucky. Or they have loads of experience in the tech-world, or in huge marketing positions. And that gives them a leg up."

Beth swallowed hard, her enthusiasm almost instantly dampened. "I know."

"It's not that I don't believe in you. You're a great writer. You know that. But it doesn't have to be your job. It's okay for it to be a hobby. Not everyone can be making millions of dollars and living in luxury. Sometimes, you just have to start slow, work hard, and be content with–"

"I know." She'd heard this lecture before. Harry was, quite probably, the most risk-averse person she knew. It wasn't that he didn't want her to do what she loved, it was that he didn't want her to be disappointed if it didn't work out. Steady, reliable, safe. That was Harry's philosophy.

"Listen," she said, looking out of the window and slipping her phone back into her pocket. "Do I have time to run and get food?"

"You didn't eat breakfast?"

She bit her lower lip guiltily; somehow Harry always managed to make her feel chronically disorganised.

Harry glanced at his watch. "You head inside. I'll go across the road and get you a coffee. And one of those oatmeal pots you like." He kissed her again, and this time she leaned in to it.

"Thanks."

Harry smiled, patted the steering wheel, then nodded towards the office. "Chop-chop. *I* can get away with being late..."

"But us lowly sales assistants can't?"

Harry laughed. "Sad, but true."

9

Watching him stride across the road, Beth inhaled slowly and told herself for the tenth time that morning that whatever doubts she was having about Harry would subside. It was just a phase.

She was still watching him, bracing herself for the day ahead, when a voice jolted her back to reality.

"Love's young dream… he does look good in a suit, I'll give him that."

"Morning, Jo."

"You coming inside? Or waiting for Prince Harry?" Beth's closest friend, and biggest Harry-sceptic, Josephine York, sucked in her cheeks and waved her perfectly manicured fingers at the glass door behind them.

"I'm coming. Harry's just getting me breakfast."

"Because he wouldn't let you eat in his posh-mobile?"

"No… well, yes." Before she could stop it, laughter bubbled up in her throat and she looped her leather-jacketed arm through Jo's. "I wish you wouldn't be so mean to him."

"I'm sorry. I'll work on being nicer."

"No you won't."

"No. I won't."

CHAPTER TWO

*C*ooper's Luxury Travel was located in a large, pretty from the outside but stagnant on the inside, building in the centre of town. The downstairs, where clients were welcomed with velvet couches and Nespresso coffee, was out of bounds to the telesales staff like Beth and Jo. They weren't even really supposed to enter through the front, but if they arrived before Helen Cooper – the great-granddaughter of the original Bernard Cooper – they often braved it. Sometimes, Jo even swiped them a mug of Nespresso on the way.

Harry's desk was opposite Helen's in the big open plan downstairs office. He was her second in command, and Beth had always been convinced that he had a bit of a crush on her. Not that he'd ever pursue it; Harry wasn't that kind of guy. But it irritated Beth all the same.

Helen was tall and athletic. She wore high heels, and bright red lipstick, and when she thought no one was looking she perched on the edge of Harry's desk and laughed loudly at his jokes.

The upstairs of Cooper's was nothing like the downstairs. It was dark, low-ceilinged and beige. Beige carpets, beige walls, beige chairs and barely a flicker of natural light. It made Beth feel as if she was living in a hamster cage with a tablecloth draped over it, but Jo didn't seem to care. Her desk was littered with mugs, fake flowers, photographs and garish ornaments. Beth's, on the other hand, looked as if it was the desk of a temp rather than an employee of six years.

Raising her eyebrows in Beth's direction, Jo waved at her computer screen and said, "Have you ever noticed that you look like you're ready to walk out of the door at any second?"

"Hmm?" Beth was frowning at her computer, which was performing its traditional Monday morning longer-than-usual warm up routine.

"You look like you're all packed up and ready to leave."

Beth grimaced. "I wish I was."

"Shhhh." Jo widened her eyes and lowered her voice. *"The powers that be* might hear you."

Finally, the computer whirred into life and Beth began checking through her bulging inbox. By nine twenty, she'd cleared all of the easy to answer emails and had a list of ten more complex queries that would take the rest of the morning to deal with. Her coffee and oatmeal pot still hadn't materialised, so she opened her desk drawer and broke into a chocolate bar. She was mid-bite when a shadow crossed her screen and Helen's crisp, nasal voice said, "Beth, when you've finished your... snack. Could you join me downstairs at my desk?" She said 'snack' as if Beth was chomping her way through a double cheeseburger and fries, and washing them down with a triple-chocolate milkshake.

As Helen clip-clopped away, Jo leaned over and whispered, "Uh oh. What did you do?"

Beth stood up, suddenly lacking the appetite for the chocolate, brushed her hands on her jeans and straightened her mustard-yellow sweater. "No idea."

"Well, be careful. The vampire looks hungry…" Jo made pretend-fangs with her index fingers and stuck out her tongue. Beth couldn't remember where the nickname 'vampire' had come from, but she felt like 'black widow spider' was probably a more fitting description for Helen Cooper.

Downstairs, crossing from the elevator towards Helen's desk, Beth glanced over at Harry. He was mid-conversation with a shiny haired couple who were holding hands and poring over brochures of the Maldives. He was good at talking to happy couples. Somehow, he knew exactly the right things to say to persuade them to add on a few expensive extras without seeming sleazy or as if he was trying too hard.

Helen didn't look up when Beth sat down, just carried on clicking her mouse and chewing her lower lip until Beth cleared her throat and said, "You wanted to talk to me, Helen?"

"Beth, yes." Helen looked up and pushed her keyboard

away from her. "I wanted to give you a heads up because Human Resources are going to be having a word with you."

"HR?" Beth felt her buttocks tense as she shifted in her chair.

"Yes." Helen paused and pursed her lips. Then, dramatically, as if she was revealing that Beth had been hiding a secret career as an adult film star, she turned her screen outwards. Open in her browser was the home page of Beth's blog. "You didn't mention that you were a writer."

Beth narrowed her eyes, noticing that the 'featured' articles that should display on the right-hand side were, for some reason, not showing and making a mental note to investigate when she got home. "Yes."

Helen cleared her throat, turned the screen back, and shook her head. "Did you ask permission from myself or another senior member of staff before starting this venture?" Helen glanced over Beth's shoulder at Harry.

"I wouldn't exactly call it a 'venture'– I'm yet to make any money from it." Beth laughed, but Helen simply blinked slowly at her.

"But you hope that one day it will?"

Suddenly feeling as if she was about to be tricked into saying something she'd regret, Beth shrugged and crossed her left leg over her right knee. "Oh, I doubt it. It's just for fun, really."

"Nevertheless," said Helen, tightly. "Did you ask permission?"

"I wasn't aware I needed to." Beth looked at Harry,

wondering whether he'd be in trouble for not reporting her clandestine blogging activity.

"Well, yes, I'm afraid so. Your contract clearly states that you're not to undertake any other kinds of work... I forget how it's phrased exactly... but you're especially not allowed to do anything related to what we do here at Cooper's."

Beth swallowed hard, disbelief rising in her throat. "I'm not starting up a rival agency, Helen. It's a travel blog. That's all." She should be holding her tongue but she'd never been very good at that.

Helen stretched her lips into a smile that exposed too much gum. "I know. And I'm sure it'll turn out to be perfectly within the rules of your employment but, nevertheless, you understand that I had to pass the matter over to HR. And that they might need to ask for some clarification from you?"

"Clarification about what?"

Helen waved her hand as if it was insignificant, already turning back to her computer. "Just making sure you haven't used any of the company's time or resources. Like I said, I'm sure it will be fine."

Beth laced her fingers together and through gritted teeth said, "Will that be all?"

Helen nodded and made an *mmm* sound. As Beth crossed back towards the elevator, she tried to catch Harry's gaze but he didn't look in her direction and by the time she got back to her desk she was seething.

"What happened?" Jo mouthed at her, resting the phone

on her shoulder mid-conversation and allowing whoever was on the other end to talk to no one.

Beth shook her head, tucked herself back under her desk and tried to focus on her to-do list but when lunch finally rolled around she practically dragged Jo out of the back of the building.

"I need to get out of here."

"Costa?"

"No, Harry will come looking for us. Let's go to Baxter's."

Jo wrinkled her nose. Baxter's was small, cramped, and the coffee was dreadful. But she followed Beth anyway and, as soon as they were safely ensconced in the corner with their limp salads and weak teas, she placed both palms purposefully on the table and said, "Well? What happened?"

Beth sighed and scraped her fingers through her hair. She repeated what Helen had said, and Jo audibly gasped and clapped her fingers across her mouth. "But they can't stop you from having a hobby. That's nonsense."

Beth bristled and sat up straighter. "It's not a hobby—"

"Yes, but they don't know that."

"She said something about me using the company's resources."

"And have you?"

Beth shrugged. She'd been wondering about it all morning. "I mean, I've worked on it in my lunch breaks. And Charles, from Fitzgerald's, gave me some samples of their new walking boots to review. But..." she sighed and shovelled a fork full of lettuce into her mouth. "Oh, I don't know. Helen hates me. So, even if I haven't done anything wrong, she'll probably engineer it to look as if I have."

"But she can't fire you, can she?"

"I suppose it depends on what it says in my contract."

"Didn't you read it?"

Beth widened her eyes and tutted. "Yes. But I've been here six years. I don't remember what was in it. I don't even know where it is. Would you know what was in *your* contract?"

"Well, no," Jo replied. Then, after a pause, she added. "But Harry won't let her get rid of you. He'd never..."

"I'm not so sure. He's desperate for a promotion. He won't do anything to jeopardise it. And it sounds like *he* could be in trouble for not telling Helen about it."

"But he'd stick up for you, surely? He wouldn't let Helen..."

Beth looked down at her plate, then sat back and folded her arms in front of her chest. "I don't know. He's not a fan of the blog. He thinks it's a waste of time."

"Well then maybe this is a sign."

"A sign?"

"That it's about time you decided whether you're going to go for it and be a famous travel-writer-blog-sensation. Or..."

"Or?"

Jo shrugged and raised her thick dark eyebrows. "Or accept your fate, grovel to Helen, marry Harry, and work at Cooper's for the rest of your life."

Beth laughed nervously. But, although she knew Jo was exaggerating, she really did feel as if she was being pushed towards making a decision. A decision she wasn't anywhere near ready to make.

"Well?" Jo was still looking at her with both eyebrows tweaked comically upwards, the way she did when she wasn't going to give in.

"What? You want me to decide now?" Beth laughed and shook her head.

Jo slurped her tea. Then reached for her phone and slid it across the table. "Maybe this will help you decide. It's a competition. I think you should enter."

Before even looking, Beth knew what Jo was showing her: Nomad, one of the biggest names in the business – a travel agency with offices all over the world – were just about to close a competition that had been plastered all over social media for months. Every year for as long as Beth could remember, they offered the chance for one lucky travel writer to win sponsorship from Nomad, and a ticket to travel around the world, all expenses paid, for an entire year. Blake O'Brien had entered it and he'd posted his piece on his blog, although Beth had no idea why he even needed to when he was already making a living from his work and travelling all over the place.

Blake O'Brien's article was the precise reason Beth had decided not to enter; against writers like him, she had absolutely no chance of winning.

"It's made for you. It says right here, the judging is

anonymous so it's not about how many stupid followers you have or how big your platform is, it's just about the writing. And you," Jo reached out and squeezed Beth's hand, "are an amazing writer, Beth Greenwood."

Beth shook her head, but despite herself she was already wondering, *What if?*

"It closes tomorrow. I don't have time," she said weakly.

"So? I'll tell the girls in the office that you got a stomach-ache. Go home. Write something this afternoon. One thousand words about what inspired you to be a travel writer. That's all you need."

Beth breathed in sharply through her nose. "My dad inspired me."

Jo smiled. "Then it shouldn't be too hard to write, should it?"

CHAPTER THREE

THREE WEEKS LATER

*B*eth's phone was buzzing. Buzzing. Buzzing. She glanced at the clock. It wasn't even five-thirty in the morning. Without looking at the caller ID, she held her phone to her ear and mumbled, "Harry? It's way too early..."

"Miss Greenwood?" A smooth, female voice. "My name's Emily and I'm calling from Nomad World Travel."

Beth blinked hard and pushed herself up on her pillows. "Yes, this is Beth." Her chest felt tight. A little tiny jumping-up-and-down voice in her head was whispering:

They don't telephone runners up. This means something. Hold on tight...

"I'm sorry to call so early. The time difference is tricky."

"It's no problem, honestly."

"Great, so you've got a minute to chat?"

"Of course." Usually it took at least two coffees for Beth to feel awake, but all of a sudden she was tingling and wide-eyed.

"Excellent. Well, I'm sure you've guessed that I'm calling about our travel writing competition?"

Beth swallowed hard but couldn't make any sounds come out of her mouth.

"Usually, we narrow the entries down to three finalists and then we get them to write another, commissioned, piece. But, as you know, this year we're doing things a little differently."

"Differently?" Beth hadn't even read as far as the 'What Happens Next' section in the entry guidelines. She'd just typed her one-thousand words, said a prayer, and emailed it off into cyber space, assuming that would be the end of it.

"This year, we're only selecting two finalists and, this is the really exciting part, those two finalists are going to be sent on a very special trip. They're going to be asked to blog about their journey and, at the end of it, the best blogger will win." Emily really did sound excited.

"That's..." Beth's heart was pounding.

"Beth?"

"Mm hmm?"

"We've selected you as one of our finalists."

"I..."

"Congratulations!"

"I don't know what to say."

"Well, what I need you to say is that you're going to be

available for a two-week trip across Canada, leaving in a month's time. May 1ˢᵗ. Can you do that?"

"Canada?" Beth could hardly believe what was happening, and she couldn't sit still any longer. Leaping out of bed, she started to hop up and down. "Yes! Absolutely! Of course!"

"Fantastic! Well, listen, I'll let you go shout about the good news and I'll email you over our terms and conditions, the itinerary, and the contact details of the other finalist in case you guys want to be in touch before you set off."

"Thank you. So much."

"Beth, it's our pleasure. Your piece was fantastic. And I wish you lots of luck with the final phase of the competition."

After putting down the phone, Beth got ready for work in a daze. Mum was already at the hospital for an early shift and without someone to squeal and shout with, she felt suddenly overwhelmingly nervous. This was huge. The biggest thing that had ever happened to her. It could change her entire life – but was she ready?

All the way to the office, she barely spoke. And Harry watched her intently, constantly glancing at her from the corner of his eyes, clearly convinced she was having some kind of breakdown.

Finally at her desk, she quickly opened up her emails and

there at the very top of the list of unread mail was the message Emily had promised her.

Instructions For Finalists.

Congratulations!

You have been selected as one of just two finalists in this year's Round the World Travel Writer's Competition.

You and your fellow finalist will be competing to win an all-expenses paid round the world trip (you will be permitted to take a friend or family member of your choice), sponsorship for your blog, and $10,000 spending money.

For this final part of the competition, you will embark on a two-week train journey across the beautiful country of Canada, starting in Vancouver and ending in Toronto. You will be accompanied by a Nomad member of staff, all food and accommodation will be paid for, and we'll give you a daily allowance of one-hundred Canadian dollars for the duration of the trip. We will be asking you to submit one blog entry every two days, talking about your experiences. You will be judged on your blog's popularity, the strength of your writing, and your personal style.

Full instructions, terms and conditions, itinerary and competition rules are attached to this email. Please confirm within 24 hours that you are able to travel to Vancouver on May 1st.

Best wishes,

Emily

Beth was re-reading the email with her mouth slightly open when Jo pinched her shoulder and whispered, "What on earth are you reading? You've barely looked up since you got here..."

Beth, still speechless, tilted her screen towards Jo and allowed her fingernails to grip the desk in front of her. Twenty-four hours. She had twenty-four hours to decide.

As Jo read the email, Beth watched her friend's face become more and more flushed and eventually Jo let out a tiny squeak, grabbed Beth by the arms, hauled her up out of her seat and yelled across the office, "This woman, ladies and gentleman, is a genius!"

All around her, colleagues looked up from their desks with raised eyebrows and curious grins.

"She's only gone and made the final of the Nomad competition!" Jo said it before Beth could stop her, and suddenly the entire office was crowding around, peering at the email, hugging, jostling, congratulating.

"Well, I haven't decided if I'm going to..." Beth began to speak but Jo pressed a finger to her lips and said, "Don't you dare. Of course you're going."

"But..."

"Beth Greenwood, this is the chance of a lifetime. There's no way I'm letting you turn it down."

"You really think I should...?"

"Beth. You could *win* this. It could change your life." Jo was grinning – a true, ecstatic, so wide it was probably hurting her cheeks kind of grin.

Her enthusiasm was infectious, and Beth's nerves started to melt away, replaced by a tingling sense of pride and excitement. Then, just as she was about to shoo everyone away, sit down and reply to Emily with a big fat YES I ACCEPT, the room started to hush.

"Am I interrupting something?"

Helen.

Beth's colleagues instantly started to scurry back to their desks, until it was just her and Jo lingering in the middle of the room.

"Helen..." Beth glanced at Jo, and Jo nodded at her. She had no choice. She had to tell her boss what was going on.

Beth swallowed hard. "Helen, I have some news. I've been selected as a finalist in Nomad's travel writing competition."

Helen's eyebrow twitched. "A finalist? This is with your blog I assume?"

Beth nodded. "Well, sort of." She paused and then, like ripping off a band-aid, as quickly as possible she said, "I'd have to travel to Canada for two weeks on May 1st."

Helen narrowed her eyes and bit the corner of her lip. "Then I assume you'll be handing in your notice?"

Beth's muscles tensed. She lowered her voice. Everyone was watching. "Well, actually, I was hoping that maybe we could arrange some unpaid vacation time?"

Quick as a flash, Helen replied, "I don't think that will be possible. To be honest, Beth, this is probably for the best. HR really aren't happy about you pursuing your blog business while working here, and this way will be much better for you. Handing in your notice to take part in a competition looks much friendlier on the CV than being fired for misuse of company resources."

Beside her, Jo stepped forward and Beth could tell that her friend was about to say something, so she grabbed her arm and squeezed a little.

Sucking in her breath, straightening her skirt, and flicking her hair over her shoulder, Beth decided that, for once, she wasn't going to allow herself to be bullied. And before she could stop herself, she raised her voice and replied, "Helen? You are absolutely right. I quit."

Helen's smile wavered, then fell into a pursed ugly line. "I beg your pardon?"

Beth leaned forwards then, louder still, and with all the gusto she could muster, she repeated, "You can stick your job, and Human Resources, and your terrible holiday allowance where the sun doesn't shine. I QUIT."

CHAPTER FOUR

*B*eth didn't look at Jo, or at anyone else, as she stomped proudly out of the building. She felt like a movie star. She had done what every person since the beginning of time had wanted to do at one point or another; she had told her obnoxious boss: *I QUIT.*

It felt amazing. It felt freeing, and empowering, and like the start of a whole new chapter.

For approximately thirty seconds.

By the time she reached the end of the car park, she realised she'd left her handbag and mobile phone behind at her desk and descended into a state of unparalleled panic.

Was it even legal to just walk out of your job? Could they force her to work her notice period? Would Helen sue her? And Harry... Harry would be furious. He'd been in a meeting when she stormed out, so he hadn't seen her leave, but the second he emerged Helen would tell him exactly what had happened.

Beth hadn't even told Harry she'd entered Nomad's competition, let alone won it. And now she'd quit her job, made a huge scene in front of everyone, and quite possibly damaged his chances of promotion forever.

Without thinking, Beth crossed the road, not looking over her shoulder in case Helen was running after her, and ducked down the side street that led to Baxter's

Inside, she glanced at the clock on the wall behind the counter. An hour until lunch. She must have been looking on the verge of tears because Ambrose, the manager, waved her into a seat near the window and brought her a cup of tea. "On the house," he said soothingly. "Are you alright Miss Beth?"

"Could I borrow your phone Ambrose?"

"Of course," he nodded, handing her a battered Nokia that looked about twenty years old.

Luckily, she knew the Sales Department's phone number off by heart. When she got through, she asked for Jo, trying to disguise her voice but not doing a very good job.

"Beth?" Jo hissed into the phone. "Where are you?"

"I can't believe I did that."

"Me neither. But it was brilliant! Helen's face..."

"Jo, what have I done?"

"Calm down. Where are you? I'll bring your stuff."

"At Baxter's."

"I'll be there in twenty minutes. Stay put and don't, whatever you do, start regretting quitting. This is the best thing you've ever done."

For well over twenty minutes, Beth drank tea after tea, with far too much sugar, and tried to calm herself down.

By the time Jo arrived, Beth had passed blind-panic and was only mildly panicked. But when Jo told her that Harry was *furious,* she started to feel nauseous all over again.

"What did he say?" Beth was gripping her phone but hadn't dared open it to see if Harry had sent her any messages.

"Not much. But you know when he goes all sort of *red* around the edges?"

Beth buried her head in her hands. "He's never going to forgive me for this."

Quietly, Jo put her hand on Beth's knee. "Do you want him to?"

"What do you mean?"

Jo shrugged. "Harry's hardly going to give up his job and travel around the world with you, Beth. Maybe this is a sign that things aren't meant to be. Maybe it's time to..."

"Jo, I haven't *won* the competition. I'm just a finalist. And I'm not going to abandon Harry after everything he's done for me."

"Yes, but..."

Beth shook her head. "Listen, I know you don't like him. But he's been good to me. So, whatever happens, Harry and I will work it out. *If* I win, then I'll deal with it. But right now, I just need to apologise and try to persuade him that me going away for two weeks isn't the end of the world."

Jo bit her lip and made a *hmm* sound.

Beth sighed. "And then there's Mum."

"Your mum will be fine. She's a grownup."

Beth scratched her nails on the ratty fabric of the armchair she was sitting in. She should be feeling excited. But all she felt was fear. Fear that Harry would break up with her. Fear that her mum would be too lonely on her own. Fear that she'd win. Fear that she'd lose and let everyone down...

And if she was feeling like this *now*, how would she feel if she actually did win and had to go away for a year?

As Jo went to fetch more tea and some large chocolate cookies, Beth swiped open her phone. Three missed calls from Harry, a text asking her to call him ASAP, and a second email from Emily.

Hi Beth, so sorry, I forgot to give you the details of the other finalist. He's already accepted his place and is keen to talk to you before you meet in person. His email is BlakeO-Brien@thecanadianwanderer.com.

Blake O'Brien? *The* Blake O'Brien? That's who she'd be up against?

Beth smiled and closed her eyes. Competing with Blake, there was no way she'd win. And, suddenly, she felt calmer.

Without the thought of having to leave home for a year to travel the world if she actually won the competition, the trip to Canada became a whole different prospect; just two weeks with no expense, visiting a beautiful country. Plus, the chance to meet a successful blogger and learn from his expertise.

Putting it that way, Harry might even be pleased for her. So, with only a little hesitation, she replied:

Thanks Emily. Count me in! Beth. x

As expected, Mum was over the moon when Beth told her. She was even delighted that Beth had quit. "It's about time, that place was no good for you. You're so much better than Cooper's. Dad and I always said so."

Harry, on the other hand, was not over the moon. He simply sat, on the edge of the sofa, perched there as if he didn't want to allow himself to become comfortable, frowning and shaking his head.

"Harry, I'm sorry I didn't tell you that I entered. I didn't think it would come to anything..."

"Do you know how ridiculous you've made me look, Beth? When Helen told me you'd quit to go take part in a competition, I had no idea what she was talking about. *She* had to explain to *me* that my girlfriend was leaving the country." He sighed and wrung his hands in his lap. He was sitting with his knees pressed together in a way that Beth always found slightly irritating. "I feel like I don't even know you anymore."

Beth sat down beside him and took his hand in hers. "Harry, don't be like that. Of course you do. You know how important my writing is to me."

Harry's temples had started to turn red and Beth got the feeling he was trying to stop himself rolling his eyes.

"Look, Harry, I'm not going to win. I'm up against Blake O'Brien. He's already got a great blog. So, if they're looking for someone to sponsor, he's got it in the bag."

"Then why bother going? Why chuck in your career at Cooper's for nothing?"

"I think *career* is a bit of an overstatement, don't you?"

"Plenty of people work their way up from the Sales Department to become management. You know that. And there's talk of a new branch... I thought you and I could..." Harry paused and chewed his lip. "I'll talk to Helen. When the dust has settled, I'll..."

"Harry, I don't want to work at Cooper's for the rest of my life."

"So then what will you do?"

"I'll go to Canada. It'll be an amazing experience, even knowing I won't win."

"And then what?"

Beth tried not to blink at the fact that, not once, had Harry said, *Don't be so defeatist,* or, *Have faith in yourself Beth,* or, *You're an amazing writer, Beth, of course you could win,* or even, *I'm not sure I like the idea of you being travel compan-*

ions with a famous and very good looking Canadian guy for two weeks. "Well," she said, "then I'll figure something out."

For at least an hour, their conversation went round and round and round. Until, eventually, Harry conceded defeat. Reluctantly, he agreed it would be nice for Beth to see Canada by train – the way her father had always wanted to – and not to say anything to Helen about potentially returning to Cooper's until Beth had thought about what she wanted to do in the future.

As he left, he kissed her on the cheek – his cheek kisses were always a little sloppier than she was comfortable with – and said, "I care for you, Beth. So much. I just want what's best for *us*, as a couple. You know that, don't you?"

Beth nodded and patted his arm. "I do. You've always looked after me." And he had. Always.

Inside, she closed the door and leaned against it. Then, feeling slightly guilty but not entirely sure why, she took out her phone and opened her emails.

Dear Blake,

Thanks for giving Emily your contact details to pass on to me.

I'm not nearly as well travelled as you and my blog is just a fledgling compared to yours, so this is all pretty daunting.

I've been a fan of your website pretty much since you started it, so I'm really looking forward to meeting you, and to two weeks in your beautiful home-country.

Best wishes,

Fellow Finalist, Beth Greenwood.

As she pressed send, Beth wondered for a moment whether she'd sounded a little *too* fan-girly. But she shrugged it off. Blake O'Brien didn't seem like the kind of guy who would judge her for trying to be open and friendly. He seemed like exactly the kind of person she could learn a lot from and, suddenly, she couldn't wait to get on the plane.

CHAPTER FIVE

ONE MONTH LATER
Day One, Vancouver

From Vancouver airport, Beth was whisked directly to the fanciest hotel she'd ever stayed in. It was six a.m. Vancouver-time, which for Beth was past lunch time, and she was both starving hungry and exhausted from the flight.

Flopping down into a large leather armchair in the hotel lounge, she rubbed her tongue over her fuzzy-feeling teeth, remembered the pale freckled-skin that had stared back at her in the bathroom mirror of the arrivals hall, and wished she'd had the foresight to pack some makeup in her hand luggage. She was smoothing her flyaway brown hair and trying to look a little more like an experienced traveller when a tall blonde woman in a pencil skirt and high heels trotted across the marble floor towards her and greeted her with a hug.

"Beth, it's great to finally meet you. I'm Emily. From Nomad's Toronto office. I'll be accompanying you guys on your trip." For some reason, everything she said sounded like a question.

Beth blinked quickly, trying to make her brain catch up. "You're British? I hadn't realised. On the phone you sounded more Canadian..."

Emily chortled and tossed her hair over her shoulder. "Well, I've lived in Toronto for... oooh... seven years now."

Emily sat down opposite and waved for a member of staff to bring them some coffee. "Now, I know you're exhausted from your trip, so I'm going to make this brief. You've read the itinerary, and you attended the induction at the London office?"

Beth nodded. She'd made the trip to London two weeks ago to sign paperwork and go over the particulars of the competition, although she deliberately hadn't looked too closely at the itinerary; she always preferred to discover things on the way rather than research and plan beforehand.

"Great. So, you know that things are going to be pretty tightly scheduled... to make the competition fair, you and Blake will be doing most things together. You'll do the same activities, visit the same places, and every two days you'll each submit a blog post that will be uploaded to our website."

Beth breathed in deeply and tugged at her sweater. They'd been through all of this in London and it had made her realise that the trip was actually going to be *a lot* of work. Not quite the leisurely trip she'd first pictured, but exciting nonetheless. And, despite telling herself that she was there just for a vacation, she was already starting to feel a twinge of competitiveness in her belly.

"This morning is all yours to recover from your flight, acclimatise, eat, freshen up," Emily continued, flicking the screen on her iPad to an hour-by-hour schedule. "Then at one p.m. we're going to meet back here. I'll introduce you to Blake, we'll do a quick video interview with you both, and then we'll head to Granville Island for the market. It's adorable. You'll love it. Tomorrow, it's Lynn Canyon Park in the morning, and in the afternoon I'd recommend working on your first article. We'll need that submitted by midnight tomorrow. Okay?"

"Tomorrow. Midnight. Got it." Beth was very glad they'd included all of this in the orientation pack because her head was groggy and she was struggling to focus.

"We leave Vancouver on Monday morning and board the train for the Rockies. But, don't worry, I'm going to be with you guys the whole way. I'll keep reminding you where we're going next and where you're supposed to be. So, don't feel like you have to remember all this!"

Finally, the coffee arrived and Beth smiled as she took a large sip. "Thanks Emily. I appreciate it."

"No problem." Emily smiled broadly and drank her own coffee – an espresso in a miniature cup – in one mouthful.

"Okay, I should head off. When you're ready to go up to your room just let reception know."

Beth nodded. Then, just as Emily was about to walk away, Beth raised her hand, as if she was still in school, and tentatively asked, "Emily, is Blake in this hotel too?"

"Oh sure," said Emily. "But he arrived last night, so he's gone off to explore the city. He and I were on the same flight from Toronto. He's a great guy, you'll love him. See you soon." And, with that, she was gone.

Seven hours later, Beth was woken by a loud, slightly frantic, knocking on her hotel door. Stumbling out of bed she pulled the door open and squinted at the brightness of the hallway.

"Beth? It's one thirty. We were expecting you downstairs half an hour ago?" Emily was smiling, but nervously checking her iPad schedule at the same time.

Beth glanced at her watch, then grabbed her phone from the bedside table and shook it. "I'm sorry Emily, the battery must've died. I set an alarm—"

"It's okay." Emily was shaking her head, clearly trying to make her feel better. "Don't panic, but we better get going..."

Beth looked down at her crumpled clothes. Her jeans were okay, but her sweater was creased and not really appropriate for what looked like a warm sunny day outside. "Could I have a moment? I'm so sorry. I'll be quick."

"Ten minutes? I'll wait in the lobby."

Beth scurried to her case and threw it open, grabbing a plain white t-shirt and her makeup bag. She applied a smattering of eyeliner and some mascara. But her hairbrush was unfindable, buried somewhere beneath two weeks' worth of packing, so she simply ran her fingers through the tangles and hoped that everyone would assume this was her look: effortlessly casual.

Downstairs, Emily was leaning against the reception desk and tapping her foot on the floor. But Blake O'Brien was nowhere to be seen.

"Blake went on ahead," she said, already trotting towards the big glass doors that led out onto the street. "I called a cab. We'll catch up with him at the Aquabus dock and do the interview on the boat over."

Beth's stomach tightened; she was already messing up. She hadn't turned up in Vancouver expecting to be able to beat Blake, but she'd intended to at least prove she was a worthy finalist. She'd pictured herself confidently shaking his hand, unfazed by the fact that he'd never replied to her email, and speaking knowledgeably to him about travel and writing and the latest trends in the industry.

Instead, she'd overslept, made them late, forgotten her camera, and her reflection in the cab's windows told her she looked like a deer caught in headlights.

As they approached the dock, however, and she caught sight of the waterfront for the first time, her nerves started to fade. The sky was bright and dimpled with white fluffy clouds, and bobbing in the water a small boat with a yellow roof and a rainbow coloured banner on its side waited for them to board.

Beth grinned, and caught Emily watching her.

"I suppose it's very British of me to think this is really quaint and lovely?"

Emily shrugged and smiled at the boat too. "I've been to Vancouver heaps of times, but the Aquabus is still my favourite part. You'll love Granville Island. It's adorable."

"It's really popular with artists, is that right?"

They were climbing out of the cab and Beth was waiting for Emily's answer when a deep, unfamiliar voice chimed in. "It certainly is. A hub of creativity, bright colours, great food..."

Beth turned around a little too quickly and the movement made her wobble.

"You must be Beth Greenwood. *Fellow finalist*. I'm Blake O'Brien." Blake extended his hand and offered a firm shake. "I'm glad you could make it. I was starting to think I'd be getting a head start." He was smiling but there was a glint in his eyes that told her he was poking fun at her. He'd never replied to her email, and yet he'd referenced it with his 'fellow finalist' remark. Clearly, he thought a lot of himself and not very much of her.

Beth felt her cheeks flush but she blinked away the awkwardness and took back her hand.

In person, Blake was shorter than she'd expected, but his square jaw, dark hair, smooth Canadian accent, and ridiculous dimples made up for it. He was wearing a checked red shirt with a white t-shirt underneath, and Beth hated that she was noticing how good looking he was.

Looking away from him and towards the boat, she tried to recalibrate herself. She'd met celebrities before, *real* celebrities, people much more famous than Blake – Cooper's was well known for its luxury clients – and yet for some reason this semi-well-known blogger was making her nervous.

"Shall we...?" Blake waved towards the boat and grinned at her.

"Yes, let's."

Beth strode off in front of him, taking a deep breath and reminding herself that she had earned her place in the competition. She deserved to be there. And Blake O'Brien had no right to make her feel otherwise.

CHAPTER SIX

The boat journey to Granville Island should have been idyllic. She should have been leaning over the side, marvelling at the scenery and taking pictures to send to her mum. But instead, she was standing beside Blake O'Brien with her back to the water, answering questions that she really didn't want to answer.

"So," Emily smiled broadly, motioning for Beth and Blake to stand a little closer together. Other people were watching, and Beth felt stiff and awkward. But Blake seamlessly inched towards her and slung his arm around her shoulders. "Our two finalists," Emily continued. "Beth and Blake, it is so great to finally meet you both." She was speaking loudly and in an exaggerated British accent. "How does it feel, Beth, to be here in the beautiful city of Vancouver?"

Beth desperately wanted to shrug off Blake's arm, and

she could feel her words getting mangled before they'd even made it out of her mouth. "Oh, it's fantastic." She was trying to sound cool and knowledgeable, and cute-British not posh-British. "Unbelievable actually. I can't believe that a few days ago I was in sleepy old Oxford and now I'm here. In Canada. With this view." She gestured to the Vancouver skyline behind them and Emily gave her a thumbs up.

"Are you nervous about the competition?"

Before Beth could answer, Blake gave a small throaty laugh and said smoothly, "Well, of course she is. She's up against *me*."

Beth felt the hairs on her neck standing on end. How *dare* he be so arrogant?! "Actually," she said, remembering how good it had felt when she stood up to Helen, and trying to summon some of the same courage, "I was pretty nervous on the flight over, but when I met Blake the nerves sort of disappeared." She glanced up at him, then looked straight at Emily's camera. "I guess I'm feeling more confident now I've seen my competition."

Blake blinked at her and smiled with the side of his mouth.

"Now, now," said Emily, "play nice you two."

The interview continued for a few more minutes, with Emily asking each of them about what they were most excited to see on the trip, how they felt when they heard they'd made the final, and about their writing experience prior to the competition.

As Blake regaled Emily with his CV – five years working for Toronto's biggest travel company in digital marketing before starting his own blog, moving to the city, and going from zero to making a living in just under a year – Beth took a deep breath and tried not to lose the sense of stubborn competitiveness she'd felt when he goaded her.

By the time Emily asked her the same question, however, she was starting to give in to the realisation that she had absolutely *no* experience and Blake had *heaps*. She was totally new at this. So, she did what she'd promised herself she would never do; she told Emily, and the camera, and all of Nomad's followers that her father was Charles Greenwood. Famous travel writer.

For a moment, Emily didn't blink or move. Blake, who was now leaning back against the railings of the boat raised both eyebrows.

"Really?" Emily reached for her iPad. "Did we know this about you Beth?"

"No. I've never mentioned it on my blog. And I made sure to keep his name out of my competition entry." She was already regretting it. She shouldn't have said anything.

"Right." Emily laughed nervously. "Of course. Well, that's certainly some experience right there. Did your father teach you a lot about writing?"

Beth wondered if Emily knew that her father had passed away. Pretty much everyone had heard of his most famous books, but not many people had read the tiny amount of news coverage about his death.

"Beth? Did your father teach you a lot about writing?" Emily repeated her question, slowly.

Beth shook her head and folded her arms in front of her, trying to dislodge the guilty feeling in her stomach. "I guess it was more that *he* was always writing, so that made me want to. I'd sit with him in his writing shed and scribble things while he worked." Beth suddenly pictured her mum's face as she watched the interview online and heard Beth talk about her dad. Would she think Beth had mentioned him to give herself a leg-up? *Was* that why she'd mentioned him?

As the thoughts tumbled across her mind, giving her an instant headache deep in her temples, she tried to change the subject. "But I worked at a travel company too, actually. Like Blake. So, I guess that's probably my most relevant experience. I worked at Cooper's Luxury Travel in Oxford."

Emily nodded. She was clearly more interested in talking about Charles Greenwood than she was in Beth's job at Cooper's.

Beth was trying to work out what she could say to steer the conversation in a different direction when, above them, a bell sounded. They'd reached Granville Island and so, reluctantly, Emily wrapped up the interview and put away her camera.

As they disembarked, Blake stepped up beside her and whispered, "Wow. I mean, wow. I'm a huge fan of your dad's books."

"You are?"

Blake nodded. "Listen, you know all that was just for show. The whole *I'm going to kick your butt* thing. I was just trying to be..."

Beth stopped and looked at him. He was almost impossible to read; constantly smiling, with his strong jaw and his twinkling eyes making it seem like everything was either a chat-up line or a joke. Not giving anything away. "You were trying to be...?"

"Funny?" Blake laughed a little and nudged her upper arm as if they were old friends.

"Right." She was trying to soften towards him but couldn't quite manage it. "Well, maybe I don't get Canadian humour."

Blake rubbed the back of his neck and shrugged. "That's okay. You Brits are known for being a little stuck up, aren't you?"

"At least we have the courtesy to reply when someone sends us a well-intentioned email."

Blake's eyes widened, as if he was surprised Beth had mentioned it. He opened his mouth, but nothing came out.

Beth shook her head, tutted, and walked on ahead – deliberately not looking back.

Under the huge-lettered sign that read *Granville Island Public Market*, Emily told them they'd have four hours to savour the sights and that it was their choice whether they did this together or separately. Before Blake could say anything, Beth said, "Separately, thanks, see you in four hours," and strode off along the waterfront.

She had no idea where she was going, she just knew that she needed to do this alone. Blake had somehow, in the short time she'd known him, managed to get under her skin. She wasn't sure if it was knowing that he'd received her email and hadn't bothered to reply that was getting to her, if it was because he'd been making fun of her, or if it was because he oozed with the kind of confidence that was more like arrogance. But she knew that his presence plus her travel-weary head would make it almost impossible to concentrate.

Walking beside the water, taking in the boats and the people and the sunshine, Beth felt herself start to relax a little. On a small wooden jetty, a musician was playing guitar and singing a song she didn't recognise, tapping his foot and bobbing to the backing track. She stopped and took a photo with her phone, still kicking herself for leaving her camera at the hotel. She was good at photos, and she knew from following Blake's blog that it wasn't one of his strongest points.

"Great isn't he?" A woman in a flowery dress threw some coins into the singer's guitar case and smiled at Beth.

"Really great." Beth paused, then as the woman was about to walk away, she called after her, "Excuse me. I'm sorry to bother you. Are you local?"

"I am." The woman smiled.

Beth tucked her hair behind her ear. "I wonder if you could help me... I'm writing an article about the island and I'm looking for somewhere off-the-beaten track for a coffee and something to eat. Somewhere I could recommend to my readers."

"Oh sure, my favourite place isn't far. I'll show you."

So, the friendly Canadian lady walked with Beth through the crowds of tourists, down some side-streets that Beth never would have noticed, and stopped outside a small but big-windowed coffee house.

"They do great fries." The woman, whose name was Kate, waved and continued on her way, leaving Beth feeling suddenly a little more optimistic.

Inside, she ordered an espresso and a plate of yam fries, because she'd never eaten yam before and the time-difference was playing havoc with her appetite.

She was scribbling some notes about Kate and the musician and the ambience down by the Aquadock, when the waiter arrived with her coffee.

"Fries will be ready soon ma'am." He smiled and noticed her notebook. "Not giving us a bad write-up, I hope?"

Beth sat back and put down her pen. "No, absolutely not. This place is wonderful. How did you know I wasn't just writing a grocery list?"

"I didn't." He smiled again. "But I do now."

With a twinge of pride in her voice, Beth replied, "I'm a travel-writer. Actually, I'm just trying to plan what to go see next."

The waiter's eyes widened and he waved his finger in the air. "Ah, then you might be in luck! My brother runs a small tour every afternoon..." He checked his watch. "It leaves in about twenty minutes, just outside."

Beth sat up straighter and tapped her pen on the cover of her notebook. "A tour?"

"It's fantastic. He takes a really small group, five people max, to see some artists' workshops. There are a couple of food stops too. It's a great way to see something a little different."

Beth couldn't stop herself from grinning. Blake would never have thought of this. He'd be wandering around looking at the market and all the usual tourist-spots. This was *sure* to give her a head start with their first article. "It sounds great, could you let your brother know I'll join him?"

"Sure. And I'll be right back with your fries."

The waiter's brother was called Todd. He was young, about seventeen, and running tours to help him save up some money for college. Thrilled at the idea of some publicity, he let Beth join the group free of charge, and started by heading towards a quieter area of the island.

There were only three of them, Beth and a middle-aged German couple who spoke very little English, so Beth was able to ask lots of questions and take photos as they walked. Todd was part-way through explaining how and why

Granville became known for its artists when Beth felt a hand on her shoulder.

"Fancy seeing you here."

"Blake?" Beth stopped in the middle of the path, glanced towards Todd, then back at Blake. "What are you doing? How did you know where I was?"

"I was looking for a place I saw on Trip Advisor. I spotted you and thought I'd see how you're getting on." Blake looked at Todd and the German couple then smiled ironically with the corner of his mouth. "Did you join a tour group?"

"No." She couldn't tell if he was envious that he hadn't thought of it or making fun of the idea. "Listen, I've got to catch them up. I'll see you later."

"But it's not a tour?"

Beth started walking but Blake was following her. "Okay, it is. But not the kind you're thinking of."

"What kind am I thinking of?"

She let out an exasperated sigh and put her hands on her hips. "It's not some cheesy tourist outing. It's a small group. We're visiting some artists' workshops. I'm sure it's not *your* kind of thing."

"Why wouldn't it be my kind of thing?"

"Are you trying to drive me crazy? What's wrong with you?" She could feel her voice rising in pitch, but Blake just laughed and put a hand on her arm.

"Calm down. It sounds great. I'll tag along."

"No. Absolutely not. Did you follow me from the waterfront?"

"Why would I follow you?"

"I..."

She was cut off by Todd, who'd jogged back to see what was going on. "Beth, you have a colleague who wants to join us?"

Blake extended his hand and shook Todd's warmly. "I'm Blake O'Brien. You might have seen my blog? The Canadian Wanderer?"

Todd shook his head, he clearly hadn't, but was impressed all the same. "We're just getting started Mr O'Brien. I'd be happy for you to–"

"I'd *love* to." Blake glanced at Beth, grinning, and took out his phone. Waving it, and looking pointedly at the notebook Beth had tucked under her arm, he said, "I dictate my notes. I hope that's okay?"

"Oh sure," Todd nodded. "Absolutely. Whatever you need to do."

Beth couldn't help rolling her eyes. Why was he such a show-off?!

CHAPTER SEVEN

*B*eth's plans to see a side of Granville Island that Blake had totally missed were well and truly thwarted. He stuck to their tiny tour group like glue, making the German couple laugh (because, obviously, he spoke German), flattering pretty much every artist they met, asking questions, and grinning away with his stupid dimpled smile.

He was brash, and loud, and his presence made Beth feel as if she was an intruder. Where she was awkward and nervous, Blake was self-assured and knew exactly what he was doing. Even as he was dictating into his phone as they walked between locations, his material sounded on-point and interesting and exactly the kind of stuff Nomad readers would be interested in.

But, amidst all of that, Beth noticed one thing: Blake didn't take any pictures. He was so busy entertaining everyone that he didn't once capture an image to go alongside his article. So, while Blake was busy telling the artists that their work was, "Incredible... Moving... So unique...", Beth was quietly taking photos that she *knew* she'd be able to edit into something pretty stunning when she got back to the hotel, despite the fact they were just iPhone shots.

Later that night, sprawled out on her hotel bed with her iPad, she was proved right. She had captured some beautiful images of the artists, and she'd been smart enough to take a business card for each one so she could ask permission to use the images of them and their work. It was just the writing she was struggling with.

She was reading through her notes, adding to them and highlighting important bits, when her phone started to buzz. It was her alarm. She'd promised Harry she would call him at ten p.m. Vancouver-time, which would be six a.m. in Oxford.

Beth tapped her phone screen and silenced the alarm. Then scrolled to Harry's name. Harry. Harry. For some reason, she suddenly felt exhausted by the idea of talking to him. He'd sent her three 'career idea' emails since she'd left Oxford and she couldn't stand the thought of explaining why she didn't want to train as a teacher, a nurse, or an accountant.

So, instead of calling, she texted.

Hey Harry, sorry but I'm really tired. All is good. Just need some sleep. Will try and call tomorrow. Beth xxx

Then she turned her phone off before he could text her back.

Day Two - Vancouver, Lynn Canyon Park

"Wow." Even as the word escaped her lips, she knew it wasn't enough. "That's high."

They were approaching the Lynn Canyon Suspension Bridge. Strung between the trees above a fast-moving river, it was fifty metres above the ground and Beth's legs were starting to wobble.

"You don't like heights, Greenwood?" Blake was beside her, dressed in hiking boots and, once again, a checked shirt – this time blue. It was early. Not quite eight a.m. The light in the forest was still a little hazy, and the air a little cool.

Beth pulled her cardigan closer and shuddered; she never thought she hated heights. But then, she'd never crossed a bridge that was suspended precariously in mid-air before. "Not really. But this is..."

"Yeah, it's pretty high."

When they reached the start of the bridge, they were the first there. There was no one in front of them to show them how it was done. No one to prove it was safe. Just the bridge, and the trees on the other side, and what felt like a very long way in between.

Beth stopped. She couldn't persuade her legs to move.

Blake was a few feet ahead, about to stride out onto the bridge, when he looked back. "You okay?"

"I'm fine," she replied, stiffly, forcing herself to move.

"Need a hand?" Blake held out his arm, smirking slightly, but Beth shook her head. "No. I'm fine. I can manage. I'll go first." Determined not to let him see that she felt sick to her stomach, Beth wriggled past and walked quickly onto the bridge.

As soon as her feet touched the wooden slats, she felt as if the entire structure was swaying beneath her feet. Her knees had turned to jelly.

Behind her, Blake said, "You know it's super-safe up here? In fact, you're probably safer here than you were in the cab ride over." He was beside her now, looking over the edge and down at the water. "Gee, that's some view. You seen it?"

Beth closed her eyes and breathed in slowly through her nose. She couldn't believe she was doing this. She should have said no. She should have told Emily *no way* am I going up there.

When she opened her eyes, Blake was taking a photograph of the way they'd come, and another peering over the side of the bridge.

Shoot. She couldn't not take any. So, she inched her way to the centre of the bridge and took the lens cap off her camera. Looking down at the rocks and the foaming crashing water, her hand was shaking so much she felt like she might drop it. She could almost picture it shattering and being carried away in tiny little pieces.

"Get a good shot?" Blake sidled up beside her, totally unfazed by the fact that he was dangling unnaturally high above the ground with nothing but some wooden boards between him and almost-certain death.

"Maybe. I think so." Beth put her lens cap back on. "Let's go, shall we?"

"Sure. After you." Blake held out his hand and waved towards the end of the bridge. Then, finally, after what felt like forever, they were back on solid ground.

At the bottom of the bridge, looking up at it rather than down from it, Beth felt infinitely better. Tourists were starting to appear at the top, and a family of four were standing almost dead-centre looking down at the water. The angle of the early-morning sun had turned them into silhouettes. Mum, Dad, and two children pointing at the water below. Beth quickly stopped and took a photograph. Perfect.

Beside her, Blake hadn't noticed the people on the bridge; he was squinting at a map that Emily had given them. "This way, I think." He pointed towards a boarded path through the trees.

"And that leads to the swimming hole?"

"Should do. If my map-reading skills are up to scratch."

"Were you ever a Boy Scout?"

Blake laughed and gave a sort of half-wink that caught her off guard. "Oh no, I'm far too naughty to be a Boy Scout."

Beth blinked at him. Did he mean to say that? She started to blush, then so did he.

"I mean, ah..."

Blake O'Brien was flustered. Perhaps he wasn't as cool and self-assured as he made himself out to be.

"You mean...?" She waited for him to finish, enjoying watching him feel uncomfortable and noticing that his dark brown eyes were actually flecked with the same shade of green as hers.

Blake rubbed the back of his neck and tried to stand a little straighter, as if doing so would make him taller and shrug off his embarrassment. "Let's go, shall we?" He strode off, clutching the map.

Beth smiled to herself and followed.

They were about half-way there, according to Blake's map, when her phone started ringing. Instantly, she silenced it. The jaunty, loud ringtone felt totally incongruous with their surroundings and she felt guilty for interrupting the birdsong and the greenery with a reminder of the outside world.

"Nothing important, I hope?" Blake, who had been talking into his dictaphone app, pressed pause, and raised his eyebrows at her.

Beth glanced at her phone. The notification *Missed Call from Harry* glared up at her.

"No," she said. "Nothing important."

Fifteen minutes and two more missed calls from Harry later - they arrived at the infamous Lynn Canyon Swimming Hole. Beth had purposefully *not* looked up or researched any of the places on their itinerary; she wanted her reactions to them to be raw and unfiltered. Too often, people were so aware of what they were about to see – because they'd watched videos on YouTube or seen pictures on Instagram – that the magic was taken away. And she wanted to try and inject some of that magic into the articles she wrote for the competition.

So, when she saw the glistening pool of water that was so clear and blue it looked like it was from a movie set, she gave an audible intake of breath.

Beside her, Blake sat down on a large comfortable-looking rock and breathed out a long wistful sigh. "Worth getting up early for, to be the only ones here, huh?"

"Sure is," she replied, momentarily forgetting that she didn't particularly want to be friendly towards him.

Beth set down the small backpack she'd brought with her and opened it up. From inside, she took a towel and then she started to dress down to her bathing costume.

Blake looked at her, then looked quickly away, as if he'd seen something he shouldn't have. "Ah... you're not getting in are you?"

"Of course," she replied, frowning. "You're not?"

"Heck no! It'll be freezing in there."

Beth looked at the water, then back at Blake. "But it's so beautiful. How can you not want to go in?" She was already a little cold, standing there in her black one-piece suit, and

Blake was looking at her strangely. His eyes looked... softer, like she'd surprised him and he wasn't sure what to make of it.

"You head on in. Let me know what it's like."

"Okay. Your loss. Will you take a photo?" She handed him her camera, briefly wondering whether he could be trusted with it but then shaking loose her doubts and focussing on the fact that Mum would *love* to see a picture of her swimming.

"Sure."

Beth walked towards the water's edge, and paused. There was a cool breeze in the air that was making her legs feel prickly, but she ignored it and dipped her toes in the water.

Blake was right; it was *freezing*. She glanced back at him. He waved at her and grinned. "Nice?"

"Superb," she replied. She wasn't going to back down now, so she took a deep breath and waded in.

It was like swimming through ice-water. Colder than anything she'd ever felt. But, at the same time, more exhilarating than anything she'd ever felt. Moving deeper into the pool, she started to swim properly, then turned and waved back at Blake. "Did you get a photo?" she called.

He shook the camera at her. "Got it. Maybe you should come back now?"

"I'm fine. It's great. I'll just swim a little more."

Blake got up from his rock and walked closer to the water. He said something, but she didn't hear it because she was already swimming again. Rolling onto her back she looked up at the sky. Her long hair was getting wet. Her minimal makeup was probably smudged. But she didn't care. For one beautiful moment, she didn't care.

"Beth!"

She righted herself. Blake was waving her towel at her and motioning for her to come back. It was pretty cold. But it wasn't until she was back and he was passing her the towel that she realised *how* cold.

"You've gone blue." Blake laughed a little, but his expression was one of concern.

"Blue?"

"Your lips. They're blue. It says in the flyer not to swim for too long. Even in summer it's freezing in there."

Her teeth were chattering. "But look at it..."

Blake smiled and shook his head. "Here," he said, reaching out and putting his hands on her shoulders. "You need to warm up." He rubbed her upper arms, up and down. It felt nice. His hands were big and warm, and... almost as soon as the thought crossed her mind, she stepped back. Was she blushing? Or was she too cold to blush?

"Better?"

"Yes. Good. Thank you."

Blake reached for his backpack. "I've got a sweater in here. Get back into your things and you can borrow it."

Beth nodded, confused by his totally unexpected concern, then scurried behind a cluster of trees and quickly pulled back on her dry things. Towel drying her hair, she peeked through the branches of the trees. Blake was talking to a couple of twenty-something-year-old guys who'd just arrived. They were good looking guys, but Beth found herself focussing on Blake. She'd so almost leaned into his chest. She'd wanted to. Which was crazy. She barely knew him. And what she knew about him, she didn't like! He was arrogant and sarcastic and a little bit mean. He'd gate-crashed her tour of Granville Island. He hadn't even had the decency to apologise for never emailing her back. And... Harry. What would Harry say if he saw her swooning over some brash Canadian?

Beth shook her head and breathed in deeply. *That's it*, she told herself. *I'm missing Harry. That's all.*

Clearly, she was missing Harry. Being close to Blake, and being freezing cold, had made her feel things that she didn't really feel. Obviously, it was Harry she really wanted.

Wasn't it?

CHAPTER EIGHT

*A*fter the morning's excursion at Lynn Canyon Park, and Beth's ice-cold swim, Emily escorted them back to their hotel. As soon as she was back in her room, Beth sent the picture that Blake had taken to her mum, Jo, and Harry. A group email that simply said:

Missing you all but having an amazing time. Love Beth xx

Then she settled into the comfy armchair beside the big picture window that looked down at the city and wrote her first article.

It didn't come easily. Without the heavy clunk of the typewriter beneath her fingers, her words seemed slower and less fluid. By the time she reached her one-thousand-word target, the sun was setting over the city and her stomach was starting to growl.

Opening up a blank email, she took one last look at what she'd written. Then she copied in Emily and Nomad's Online Communications Editor, attached her article – complete with the pictures that she'd skilfully taken and edited – and pressed *SEND*.

She glanced at the time. Eight p.m. Back home, Harry would be sleeping. She should call him later, she knew she should. But, somehow, she also knew she wouldn't. And she couldn't work out why.

Instead, she texted Jo.

I'm avoiding Harry. What's wrong with me? Love you. Hope work isn't too awful without me.

She added a winking emoji and a heap of kisses.

To her surprise, Jo replied almost instantly.

You're avoiding him because he's a fun-sucking loser. Love you too. Work is the same. But worse.

Beth frowned at her phone. For Jo, back in Oxford, it was the early hours of the morning.

Why are you up? It's the middle of the night. She purposefully ignored Jo's comments about Harry.

Got into a Netflix binge and couldn't sleep. Don't worry about Harry. Use the time away to clear your head. Going to get coffee and head to gym. Keep sending pics. xxx

Beth drummed her fingers on her thigh. Clear her head? She didn't need to clear her head. Things between her and Harry were fine. Absolutely fine...

Day Three, The Rocky Mountaineer

The next morning, Beth woke to an email from her mum.

Dearest Darling Beth,

Thank you for your email and for the pictures of you swimming. You look freezing cold but very happy.

All is fine here at home. I know you'll be worrying about me, but I really am okay.

Your father would be so proud of you, Beth. So, whatever happens, just do your best. Don't for a second worry about what I'll do if you win and end up jetting off around the world. I'm a big girl and I have friends who would keep me busy. You never know, I might even finally leave the country and come visit you at one of your stops.

Go chase your dreams baby girl,

Love you forever,

Mum xxx

As Beth read her mother's words, she blinked quickly, wiping her watery eyes with the back of her hand. It was as if her mum knew exactly what she needed to hear. And, suddenly, thinking of the train journey she was about to embark on and the days ahead, Beth felt full to bursting with the desire to actually *do this* – to write some incredible pieces and kick Blake O'Brien's butt.

The taxi Emily had ordered arrived before seven and whisked Beth and Blake straight from the hotel to the train station where they were finally due to board the world-famous *Rocky Mountaineer* train that would take them from Vancouver to Banff. For two days – with an overnight stopover mid-way – they would travel through the breath-taking scenery of the Rocky Mountains, seeing things you could only see by rail. And Beth's skin was fizzing with anticipation.

Beside her, Blake was scrolling through his social media channels and seemed utterly unfazed by the whole experience. He was clearly travelling light, with just the small backpack he'd taken to the canyon yesterday and a similarly small wheeled suitcase. Beth, on the other hand, had her backpack, a large tan shoulder bag, and a suitcase double the size of Blake's.

As they waited on the platform for Emily to find out where they were all going, Blake eyed up her case. Sipping at the take-out coffee he was holding and barely looking up from his phone, he said, "What've you got in there? A notebook for every day of the trip? You know, most folks these days use these handy pocket-sized devices called *smart phones* for note-taking."

Beth narrowed her eyes at him. Today's shirt was red. But still checked. "I didn't get the memo about the uniform," she said, chewing her lower lip. "So, I probably over-packed."

"Uniform?"

"The checked-shirt memo. I missed it."

Blake made a *snuff* sound and looked away as if he was

trying not to laugh. Changing the subject and putting away his phone, he tilted his head towards the train. "Pretty impressive, huh?"

Beth nodded. She didn't want to talk to him, but she was finding it hard to contain her excitement. "Look at the front," she said, pointing. "I don't think I've seen a double-decker train before."

They were edging a little closer, marvelling at the deep shining blue of the carriages and the domed glass roof of the front section of the train, when Emily trotted up beside them with a porter in tow.

"Dan's going to take your luggage," Emily gestured to the porter, who took their suitcases and bags.

"I'll keep this one," Beth nudged the tan bag that was on her shoulder. "Thank you."

The porter nodded, then strapped labels to their backpacks and cases. "You'll see your bags again later today, when you stop over at Kamloops. They'll be waiting in your hotel rooms."

"They will?" Beth glanced at Blake. "If I'd known I wouldn't have to carry it far, I'd have packed a little more."

"Okay, you guys. This is where we part ways for a bit." Emily handed over her own small case and pointed at the double-tiered end of the train. "You're in the *Gold Leaf* section of the train. I'm down in *Bronze*. Dan will show you the way."

"We're up front?" Beth felt her eyes widen. She'd assumed they'd be in standard seats with everyone else.

"Didn't you read the itinerary?" Blake whispered.

Beth ignored him, waved goodbye to Emily, and then walked – in a bit of a trance – behind Dan the porter as he ushered them towards the luxury section of the train.

Almost as soon as they were seated, in big leather chairs under the large glass dome, a waiter arrived with coffee and cookies and told them to make themselves comfortable, they'd be leaving shortly.

Beside her, Blake took his phone out of his pocket and held it up to his ear. "Hey Emily. Ah ha. We're both on board." He turned and smiled at Beth. "Yep, she's right here. Yeah, we're okay. Sure. See you the other side."

"It's a bit mean that she's not up here with us. Don't you think?"

Blake shrugged. "Budget, I guess. I'm sure she's fine. 'Fraid you're stuck with me, though, until we reach Kamloops."

Beth took out her iPad and swiped open the map Emily had sent her, ignoring the little flutter in her stomach because she wasn't sure whether it meant she was *pleased* to be stuck with Blake or *not* pleased. "I haven't heard of Kamloops before," she muttered.

"There's not much there. It's just a stop-over really." He leaned over and, without asking, took the iPad from her. "See, from here to here is about three-hundred kilometres..." He looked up, clearly only just noticing that Beth had folded her arms in front of her chest and was scowling at him. Sheepishly, Blake handed back her iPad.

Beth took it and glanced behind her. Every other seat under the dome was full.

"Looking for an escape route?" Blake sipped his coffee and looked at her over the rim of his mug.

Beth shuffled a little further away in her seat. "I wanted to make notes as we travel. There's not much room to spread out, that's all."

"Just relax. Enjoy it. Looks like it's going to be a clear day. The scenery should be pretty breath-taking. Don't waste it on notes." Blake leaned back in his chair and closed his eyes for a moment.

Beth's skin prickled. "Does that mean you won't be *dictating* today?"

Blake opened one eye and smirked. "I'll give you a break from my swoon-worthy Canadian accent for a few hours, shall I?"

"Oh, please do. Which must mean you're not going to speak to me either?"

Blake was looking at her with a glint in his eye that said he was almost enjoying her answering him back, when a smartly dressed concierge appeared at the top of the stairs and waved at them all. "Ladies and gentlemen... welcome to *The Rocky Mountaineer*..."

As the train rolled out of the station, Beth felt her heart flutter in her chest. This was it. The part her father had spoken to her about so many times when they'd sat dreaming about where they'd go when he got well. Canada was, he said, the one place he wanted to go back to more than any other.

"No matter how long you're there, it's not enough to soak up the beauty, Beth." She remembered him saying it, so clearly it was as if he was right there next to her.

"Earth to Greenwood." Blake nudged her lightly with his elbow.

Beth blinked at him and tried to smile. "Just thinking about my dad," she said, surprising herself; she hadn't expected to be that open.

"Trying to conjure some of the old man's powers? What advice did he give you for the trip?" Blake paused, rubbing his square lightly-stubbled jaw. "I was wondering actually... be honest... how much did he help you with your competition entry?"

"I'm sorry?" Out of the window, trees were zipping past them in a blur, and for a second Beth thought she'd been so focussed on the view that she'd mis-heard him.

"I mean, it's okay. I'm not judging. If *my* father was a famous writer, I'd have milked him for tips too. Having said that, it's been a while since your dad published anything. What happened there? I used to read all his stuff and then it just stopped. Did he lose his publishing deal or something?"

Beth swallowed hard and folded her arms across her chest. She could feel herself trying to shrink away from him. It was her own fault; she never should have mentioned her dad in the first place. But then her guilt was replaced by a sense of indignation; how could Blake proclaim to be a fan of her father's work if he didn't even know what had happened to him?

"My father died." She didn't try to sugar coat it. She just looked Blake right in the eyes and said it, almost daring him to even *try* to make a joke of it.

Blake blinked quickly. His mouth hung open a little. "I..."

Beth looked away. Tears were coming and she didn't want him to see.

"Beth, I'm so sorry. I... I had no idea."

Still not looking at him, she sniffed and looked up at the blue sky above the dome. "It's fine. You didn't know. Let's just enjoy the trip."

"Seriously, Beth, I..."

"Don't." She looked at him this time. "Okay?"

Blake nodded. "Okay."

Thankfully, it wasn't long before the concierge told them they were approaching some stunning scenery and Beth had an excuse to stand and move towards the back of the dome. Looking out at the trees and the rivers, she understood exactly what her father had meant – it was all going by too quickly and she couldn't possibly hope to imprint it into her mind well enough for the memory to last.

Reaching for the birthstone pendant that, as always, hung around her neck, she breathed in deeply and tried to think of how she was going to write about the journey. Beside her, an elderly lady with a large camera was trying to take pictures and muttering about the glare of the sun.

"I know what you mean. I couldn't get a reflection-less shot, so I'm trying to just *remember* it now."

The woman chuckled. "Very wise, my dear."

Beth looked at the seat the woman had been in. She didn't appear to be travelling with the man next to her. "I hope you don't mind me asking," she said. "Are you travelling alone?"

"Why, yes, dear. It's a trip for solo travellers. That old fellow is Mike. Nice. But deaf as a post and not much company."

Beth glanced over her shoulder to where Blake was sitting, looking out of the window and munching on his third cookie. "I don't suppose you'd like to swap seats...?"

CHAPTER NINE

For the rest of the journey, Beth enjoyed quiet Mike and his un-intrusive companionship. Up ahead, Doris, the lady she'd swapped with, seemed to be having a lovely time talking Blake's ear off. Every now and then, Blake looked back and tried to catch her eye. But Beth didn't reciprocate.

It felt nice. Freeing. To be, relatively speaking, by herself.

Blake's presence was so... noticeable. He was always looking at her, goading her, trying to press her buttons, making jokey comments that were more like insults than humour. Always smiling, with his ridiculous Hollywood dimples and his ridiculously perfect hair.

And then just when she thought she'd got the measure of him, when she'd decided that he was most definitely a jerk, he'd soften and say something or do something that made her think she was wrong.

It was too much. She didn't need the distraction. Tomorrow, after their stopover in Kamloops, she'd ask if she could swap seats again and ride with Mike. At least then she could focus on enjoying the Rocky Mountains.

They arrived in Kamloops just as the sun was setting and, much to her annoyance, Blake was right about it being nothing very exciting. By the time they'd disembarked the train and been transferred to the hotel, it was dark outside and there was nowhere to go except the beige characterless bar downstairs.

For a while, Beth tried sitting on her bed and typing. But the words wouldn't come.

The entire day, she had felt as if she was travelling through a movie set. It was like everything she loved about England, but ten times more beautiful. Trees, blue skies, rivers, lakes, and more shades of green than she even knew existed. But she had no idea how to even begin describing it all.

Eventually, having typed precisely nothing, she gave up and went to the bar. She found a table in the corner, ordered a small glass of white wine, flipped open her iPad, and rested her fingers on the oddly smooth keyboard that had come with the case Harry bought her.

Just as she did, her phone started buzzing. She took it out of her pocket and, right on cue, was greeted by Harry's smiling face, staring up at her from the screen. It was a selfie they'd taken on her birthday. Harry had thrown her a surprise party with their colleagues from work and, even though Beth hadn't known who most of them were, it had been a lovely gesture. It was the early hours of the morning at home; he must have stayed up late so he could call her.

She paused. Her thumb lingered over the green pick-up-the-call button. But then it stopped ringing and she sighed and sank back in her chair.

A few minutes later, just as she'd finally opened up a Word document and was attempting to write, Harry called again. This time, Beth muted the call. And then a few minutes after that she muted another.

Letting out a frustrated sigh, she swigged the last of her wine and shook her head at herself.

"Who's the poor guy?" A deep, smooth, very Canadian voice jolted her out of her self-pity.

Beth looked up. Of course. Blake.

He nodded at Beth's phone. "You've red-buttoned that guy at least three times since you've been sitting there."

Beth turned her phone over so the screen was face-down on the table and shook her head. What made him so sure it was a 'guy'? It could have been anyone. "It's no one." What was she saying? Harry wasn't no one. "Just my boyfriend."

"I see." Blake nodded wisely at her and the corner of his mouth twitched into an amused smile.

"Do you?"

"I'm very astute."

Beth folded her arms and bit her lower lip. "Really? And what *exactly* have you ascertained?"

"Well, you said he was no one but then admitted he was your boyfriend. You haven't mentioned him once since we started this trip. He's desperate to talk, you're not. So, using my super-human powers of deduction, I'd say that you're on the verge of a breakup."

Beth sat up a little straighter and tapped the corner of her phone up and down on the table. She was not going to rise to the breakup comment, even though it had made her stomach twitch and her hands feel clammy. "So you've been standing around watching me for how long, exactly?"

Blake gestured to the chair opposite Beth. "Invite me to sit down, and I'll tell you."

"Fine." Beth folded back her iPad case and flicked the rim of her empty wine glass with her fingernails.

"I've been here a while. At the bar. Marvelling at your powers of procrastination."

"Procrastination?"

"Never have so few words been typed in so many minutes." He was poking fun at her again - when wasn't he? But then his expression softened and he said, "Writer's block?"

Beth sighed and gestured to her wine glass. She was too tired to keep exchanging barbs with him. "I thought this might help."

"Is it?"

"No. Definitely not."

"Want to talk about it?" He held up his hands as if she was about to accuse him of something. "I've already submitted my piece for today, so no plagiarism. I swear."

"Already?" Beth felt her eyebrows tweak upwards and knew her forehead would be showing her frown lines. "How in the world did you write it that quick?" Was he going to mention the train, or her father, or the fact she'd opted to sit beside a complete stranger instead of him?

Blake shrugged. "Practice, I guess. I used to be much slower but now I'm a content-producing machine."

"Content? That sounds very..."

"Commercial? *Un*-writerly of me?" Blake wrinkled his nose a little. "Yeah, I know. But my goal is simple – make a living from writing, travel the world. To do that, I need eyeballs on my blog. To get eyeballs on my blog, I need content. Lots of it. So, I learned to write quick."

"Don't you worry that what you write will turn out kind of shoddy?"

Blake laughed. "Yeah, but that's the difference between me and you."

"There's only one difference?"

"Okay, the *main* difference - you're clearly a perfectionist and I most definitely am not. You're trying to be a *serious* writer. But me? I'm just trying to make the big bucks." Blake leaned forward on his elbows. "The problem is, this competition isn't really about writing the kind of thing that will win a Pulitzer prize. It's about writing what people want to read.

Nomad want traffic. So, the winner is going to be the one who generates the most."

Beth sat up a little straighter. "They said it's based on lots of things..."

"Sure. They *said* that. But at the end of the day, they want clicks, just like everyone else."

"Wow." Beth breathed in sharply through her nose. "Well thanks for the depressing chat..." She stood up, tucking her iPad under her arm.

"Wait," Blake put his hand on hers, then quickly took it back. "I'm sorry. Don't go. I want to help. Really."

"Why would you want to help me?"

"Oh I don't know... to make up for being a Class-A jerk earlier on?" Blake smiled, but this time it was a small *I'm sorry* kind of smile. And when Beth still didn't sit down, he said, "Come on. I'll get us something to drink."

"Okay."

"So, what are you struggling with?" Blake had, to her surprise, returned from the bar with, instead of wine or beer, two enormous whipped-cream-covered mugs of hot-chocolate. And now he was sitting there with his hands wrapped around his mug acting as if they were friends.

"Oh, you know, just the writing part." Beth sighed, tried to laugh, and didn't manage it. "The thing is, at home I write on a typewriter. So, with this," she gestured to her iPad as if it was evil, "I just can't make the words flow."

Blake paused mid sip of hot chocolate. "You write on a *typewriter?*"

Beth felt her cheeks flush. She tucked her hair behind her ear and started to pick the miniature marshmallows out of her drink and spoon them, one by one, into her mouth.

"How? I mean, how'd you get your articles from the typewriter to your computer?"

"I do a first draft on the typewriter and then I retype them on my laptop, tidy them up and upload them to my blog."

"That's..."

"I know. Long-winded. A waste of time. Ridiculous..."

"Actually," Blake put his drink down. "I was going to say 'awesome'."

Beth frowned. "Awesome?"

"Yeah. Typewriters are cool. Very retro. And it's a nice way to separate the writing from the editing."

"I can't tell if you're making fun of me or not..."

"I'm not. I swear."

She frowned and felt herself relax a little.

"So I can see why you'd be struggling. I'm guessing the typewriter wasn't suitcase-friendly?"

"Not exactly."

"Hmm." Blake sat back and rubbed his lightly stubbled chin with his thumb and forefinger. "I've got it." He raised his hand to stop her talking and waved at the iPad. "May I?" He was being more polite this time, and Beth pushed it across the table to him. Blake flipped it open, typed something, then said, "Password?"

"I'm not telling you my password!"

"Right. Very sensible. Okay, type it in but don't look."

"Seriously?"

"Don't look," he repeated, swivelling the iPad towards her but shielding the screen so that all she could see was the keyboard. "Great. Do you have earphones with you?"

Beth reached into her bag and pulled out her wireless ear buds.

"Put them in..." Blake stood up, putting the iPad back in front of her and opening up a blank Word document. "Okay, now type..."

"What do I–?"

"Anything."

Beth wiggled her fingers above the keyboard, then gingerly typed, *Hello Blake. How are you?*

As the letters appeared on the screen, each one was accompanied by a satisfying *clunk* sound in her earbuds. The kind of *clunk* her typewriter made. The kind of *clunk* that reminded her of her father typing away into the night.

She looked up at Blake and grinned. "How did you...?"

"Just an app. Not quite the same as the real thing, but..."

"It's perfect. Thank you."

Blake shrugged, as if it was nothing, and slurped his hot chocolate. It left a moustache of whipped cream on his upper lip and Beth instinctively reached out to wipe it with her thumb. Stopping herself before she touched him, she took her hand back and gestured to her own lips instead. "You have, um... cream..."

Blake wiped at his mouth with the back of his hand, going a little cross-eyed as he tried to make sure he'd got it all. "Thanks."

For a moment, neither of them spoke. Beth tapped her fingernails on the side of her mug, then said quietly. "I'm sorry about earlier. There's no reason why you should have known about my dad. I shouldn't have reacted the way I did."

Blake, suddenly looking quite solemn, shook his head. "No. Please don't apologise. I was an *idiot*. I was trying to be clever, or funny, or something... I don't know. I was out of order suggesting he'd helped with your entry. I don't know why I said it. And I'm sorry I didn't know. I should have known. I'm genuinely a fan... it just never occurred to me..." For perhaps the first time since they'd met, he was waffling, and Beth could tell he was genuinely sorry for what he'd said.

"It's alright, Blake, really."

Blake cleared his throat and swallowed hard. "How did he... what happened?" he said, softly. His eyes were inviting her to say what was on her mind, and in her heart, but she couldn't. Maybe because she'd only just started to think of him as anything other than rude and annoying. Or maybe because if she started to talk about her dad, she'd never stop.

"Do you mind if we don't talk about it? It's just that I'm trying to focus on kicking your butt." She laughed, trying to lighten the mood. "I don't want to be distracted."

Blake bit his lower lip and his mouth spread into a smile. "Is that why you left me with Grandma Doris and went to sit with Old Man Mike? Because he's less distracting?"

"Oh absolutely. Your striking good looks are just too much to handle."

Blake held her gaze for a moment.

"Well. I should go try out this app." Beth gestured towards the lobby. "Back in my oh-so-swanky hotel room."

"You should. And I should get some beauty sleep."

In the elevator, side-by-side, alone, Beth looked straight ahead at the brushed-metal doors and found herself saying, "We're not breaking up, you know. We're good. Me and Harry." She looked sideways at Blake. His expression didn't change.

"Okay."

"He just doesn't really *get* the whole travel thing. That's all."

"He doesn't like travelling?"

"He just wants us to be secure. You know... to settle down."

"I see. And is that what *you* want?"

No one had ever asked her that before. Not Harry. Not Jo. Not her mum. No one. "I..." Beth bit her lip. "Harry's been really good to me. We've been through a lot together and–"

"That wasn't the question." Suddenly, the elevator felt very small and their bodies felt too close.

Beth tugged at the hem of her sweater. But before she

could reply, they reached Blake's floor and the doors pinged open.

"Goodnight Beth." He stepped past her, his hand brushing accidentally against hers.

"Goodnight."

The doors were sliding slowly closed when Blake turned to look at her. "Just so I know," he said, "will I be travelling with Doris again tomorrow?"

Through the now-almost-closed doors, Beth shrugged. "We'll see..."

CHAPTER TEN

*B*ack in her hotel room, Beth sat on the edge of the bed and put her head in her hands. All she could think about was Harry. But not in a good way.

Were they really on the verge of breaking up? Was that why she was avoiding his calls?

Jo had been trying to persuade her for months that she and Harry weren't 'meant to be', but Beth had always shrugged it off. Right from the start of their relationship, Jo had been hostile towards Harry because he was their boss. And because when Beth and Harry started dating it meant Jo didn't have anyone to go speed dating with anymore.

Beth had never taken it seriously. In fact, if anything, Jo's comments had always cemented the idea in Beth's mind that she should be loyal to Harry, stick up for him, make it work. Because he was a good man. But the fact that Blake – who she'd known just a few days – had picked up that there was something wrong, had made her wonder whether maybe she should start listening to Jo, and to herself.

Beth took out her notebook and flipped to a page in the back. *When in doubt, make a list.* That was her mum's motto. So, Beth created two columns.

Under *Harry – Reasons to Stick Together* she scrawled:

- *Stable*
- *Kind*
- *Reliable*
- *Attentive*
- *Loyal*
- *Supported me through dad's illness*
- *Good career prospects*

Under *Harry – Doubts* she wrote just one sentence:

- *Do we want the same things?*

Just a sentence. A much shorter column than the reasons to stick together column, but as she looked at those words – stable, reliable, attentive – she felt a tugging, twisting sensation in her stomach. Was that what she wanted? Blake had asked her outright. Straight to the point. *What do you want?* And now, sitting hundreds of miles away from Harry and staring at her list, she honestly felt as if she had no idea.

Did she want to settle down? Give up travelling? Go back to Cooper's? Get married and train as an accountant?

Or did she want to be free? Travel the world. Chase her dreams.

When she'd been using her mum as an excuse not to travel, the fact that Harry didn't want to hadn't seemed important. But now Mum had persuaded her it was okay, and she was starting to enjoy the competition, she didn't see how she could resolve things.

Suddenly, a rush of anger swept through her and she tore the page out of her notebook, crushed it into a ball and threw it towards the waste paper bin. She missed. Groaned. And flung herself back on the bed, staring at the unmoving ceiling fan.

What she wanted was the kind of relationship her parents had had. They'd been together since school and, even though her mum didn't particularly like travelling, somehow they had made something beautiful. They just *got* each other. When her father went away to write and research his books, he'd send her mother a postcard from every place he visited, and when he came home, they'd act like teenagers falling in love for the first time. Every time.

Beth glanced at the time. It was six a.m. in Oxford. She picked up her phone and dialled Harry's number.

The phone rang. And rang. And rang.

Eventually, a gruff voice on the other end muttered, "Beth?"

"Harry!" She sat up, relieved to hear his voice. "I'm so sorry I didn't call sooner..."

"I've been worried. Have you been avoiding me?"

"No. Of course not. How are things at home?"

She heard shuffling in the background. He was probably pushing himself up on his pillows, swiping his floppy red hair from his face and wiping sleep from his eyes. "Work has been difficult." His tone was clipped. He was annoyed with her.

"Oh. Because of me?"

"It's really impacted Helen's faith in me, Beth."

"I'm sorry, Harry."

"And, as for me getting you your job back, I don't think it's going to be possible. I'll make some calls, see if I can put a word in with some other travel firms. Did you look at the emails I sent you?"

Beth inhaled slowly and tried not to let herself feel annoyed. "Harry, I told you I don't know what I want to do yet. And, besides, I might win the competition..."

There was a pause on the other end of the line. And then Harry replied, "You said it was just a holiday. You said there was no way you'd win. You said you didn't *want* to win."

"I know." She was trying to pick the most diplomatic words. "But now I'm here and I'm actually *doing* it – writing, travelling, seeing these amazing things – I can't imagine coming back home and just going back to normal. And Blake. Well, he's so arrogant it's kind of made me determined to beat him."

"What are you saying, Beth? You're saying you don't want to come home?" There wasn't even an ounce of affection in Harry's voice, and Beth could picture his face turning pink around the edges as he tried not to sound angry.

"No, of course not." She sighed. Why couldn't she find the words to explain? "I just... I want to do my best, Harry. I want to try and win."

"And if you do, you're expecting me to come with you? Leave everything and travel around the world?"

"Would you?"

Without even a pause for thought, Harry guffawed into the phone. "Of course not! How could I? The new branch is opening in a few months, Beth. And despite the show you made, they're talking about making me Branch Manager."

"Right. Well, that's okay, I'll just send you plenty of postcards." She was joking, trying to be light-hearted, thinking of her parents and how they managed to still love each other and be happy even when her father travelled a lot.

"Postcards? I'm supposed to let my girlfriend go away for an entire year and rely on *postcards?*"

"*Let* me? I'm not really asking for your permission, Harry! I'm just trying to talk to you about it. Clearly you're not in the mood to listen to what I need to say."

"Beth, I always listen to what you say. Always. But you don't listen to me. I don't want to go travelling. And I don't want to be with someone who's never in the country. I know your parents did it, but quite frankly it's not normal. A husband and wife are supposed to be *together.* They're supposed to work *together* for their family. Not abandon one another and jet off around the world."

"Husband and wife? Harry we're not married." The mention of her parents, and his criticism of them, had made her blood boil and she was close to hanging up.

"Then maybe that's what you need to think about."

"What? Marriage?"

"Do you want to get married and settle down or are you going to keep chasing this dream?"

"You're asking me to choose between travelling and getting married?"

Harry paused. Then, quietly, he said, "Yes. I think I am, Beth."

"I don't want to get married." The words came out before she had the chance to stop them.

"You don't?"

There was no going back now. She had to finish what she'd started. "One day, Harry. But not now. And not–"

"Not to me." Harry finished her sentence. But it wasn't a question.

Beth scraped her hair back and blinked up at the ceiling. Tears had started to roll down her cheeks but she made no attempt to stop them.

"Harry, I..."

"Goodbye Beth. Have a good trip."

Day Four, Kamloops to Banff

The next morning, Beth woke up with her phone cradled against her stomach. She'd tried calling Harry back, but he'd refused to answer. And, eventually, he'd sent her a text message saying, *Let's talk when you get home. We both need some space to think about things. I still care for you Beth.*

She'd stopped crying after that and had eventually managed to fall asleep.

Opening the curtains to the sun rising over Kamloops and the sight of the train station in the distance, Beth sighed and deftly tied her hair back into a French braid.

She hated feeling as if she'd let Harry down, or hurt his feelings, or thrown back all the kindness he'd shown her in the time they'd been together. But, at the same time, she felt a sense of relief. She'd finally admitted it out loud, to herself *and* Harry – he wasn't the person she could imagine spending her life with. Maybe she was crazy, trying to find the kind of relationship her parents had. Maybe that kind of true love only existed in fairy tales. But she knew what her father would say. He'd tell her never to let go of her dreams. And, so far, his advice had never been wrong.

So, she packed up her bag and readied herself for the second leg of the *Rocky Mountaineer* train journey feeling weary but considerably more at peace than she had felt for a long time.

In the lobby, she found Blake and Emily standing

together near the entrance. They both looked up and waved as she approached.

"Morning, Beth." Emily hugged her briefly. "How'd you sleep?"

"Fine, thanks." Beth was avoiding looking at Blake and she wasn't sure why, but as Emily motioned towards the rail station transport outside and went on ahead, he whispered, "So, do I need to go find Doris? Or will I have the pleasure of your company?"

Beth looked at him out of the corner of her eye and tried not to smile. "You're being very polite."

"Well, I woke up this morning and decided I'd try at least one day of not being a total jerk in your presence."

"It's a little disconcerting. Makes me feel as if you're up to something."

"Geez. I can't win, can I?" He rolled his eyes, but he was smiling.

"I guess you can ride with me today."

Blake nodded. "Much appreciated."

"Seriously. Stop being weird."

"Alright. But did I tell you I like your hair today?"

Beth raised her right eyebrow – a trick she'd mastered when she was at school – and put her hand on her hip.

"Oh, okay. That's a look I don't want to see too often." Blake laughed and put his hands up as if he was expecting a poke in the ribs.

"Are you done?"

"I'm done."

Aboard the train and moving slowly out of the station, Beth and Blake sat opposite one another in the *Gold Leaf* dining car, waiting for their breakfast order of pancakes with maple syrup.

"Is Canadian maple syrup really that good?" Beth asked, waving at Mike and Doris but talking to Blake.

Blake's eyes widened as if he couldn't quite believe what he was hearing. "Ah. Yeah. It is."

"But with bacon?"

"Yeah, with bacon. You haven't *lived* until you've eaten maple syrup with bacon."

"Then I guess I've lived a very sheltered life so far."

"I guess you have. What's the best place you've travelled to?"

Beth looked down and fiddled with her napkin. "I haven't been much further than Europe, to be honest."

Blake looked up, then quickly focussed on his plate. "Don't feel bad. I haven't made it much further than Toronto since my gap year after college."

Beth frowned and stopped eating. "But... your blog? You write about India and Vietnam and New York..."

Blake cleared his throat and gave a small sheepish sigh. "Yeah. See, the thing is. That's kind of why I never emailed you back before we got here."

Beth tilted her head, waiting for him to explain.

"You seemed genuinely impressed by my writing and it made me feel a bit of a fraud. I've never been to most of those places. At least not recently. That's probably why I've been so..." He moved a half-eaten piece of pancake around his plate with his fork.

"Antagonistic?" Beth gave him the eyebrow again.

"Have I been antagonistic?"

"And rude, sarcastic, arrogant, mean..."

"Okay, okay. I get it..." Blake raised his palms at her as if he was shielding himself from an onslaught of bullets. "What I'm trying to say is that my stuff is just *content*. I've done okay. I'm making a living. But not a huge one." He shook his head and shrugged. "The irony is, I don't have the time or the money to properly travel. That's why I entered the competition. So that I can really make a go of it."

"Wow. And here was me thinking that you were *so* much more experienced than me." Beth sat back in her chair, looking at him as if all the pieces had suddenly fallen into place.

"No way. I've just got more of a strategy to what I'm doing. But your actual writing... you're good, Beth. Really good. Like, your piece on dark tourism. That blew my mind. That's *real* writing."

"You read that?" Beth felt herself start to blush.

Blake pushed his fingers through his hair and shrugged as if it was no big deal. "I discovered your blog a while back."

"I saw that you recommended my piece on hostels in Oxford, but I thought you'd just seen it somewhere online. I didn't realise you were a *fan*." Beth smiled cheekily, enjoying teasing him for once instead of it being the other way around.

"Oh yeah. The biggest. I have your picture on my wall and everything."

"Well that's just creepy."

By the time the train rolled into the small mountain town of Banff, Beth's opinion of Blake O'Brien was most definitely beginning to soften.

They still didn't see eye-to-eye on the ins and outs of succeeding as a professional blogger. But Blake was actually making a living at it, and she wasn't. So, eventually she conceded that he probably knew a little more than she did and agreed to let him give her some 'constructive' feedback on her site.

"Are you sure you have time? We've got to submit our next article by midnight," she said as they disembarked onto the platform.

"Of course. I write quick, remember?"

Beth was about to tell him it could wait until later in the trip, or even after the competition had finished, but then she looked up. And she saw the mountains. And her breath caught in her chest.

Despite the fact they'd been travelling through Canada's incredible scenery all afternoon, standing there in the fresh evening air and looking at Banff's misty mountain backdrop made her feel like crying.

"Gosh." She turned to Blake. "Can you imagine living

here? Waking up and seeing this view every single morning. On your way to work. On the way to the grocery store. How could you ever be unhappy living in a place like this?"

Blake's lips curled into a subtle smile. "You know, I don't think you could be. I think you'd be eternally, sickeningly, happy."

"I think you're right."

CHAPTER ELEVEN

Day Five, Banff

*A*s soon as she saw their Banff accommodation, Beth vowed to wake early enough to watch the sunrise over the mountains. Their rooms were in a log cabin B&B at the north end of the town, elevated above the trees so that it looked down on the Bow River below. It was everything she'd imagined when she'd thought of Banff on the way there: wood panelled walls, cosy bedrooms, and huge windows with views of the river.

At five a.m., the morning after the *Rocky Mountaineer* train pulled into Banff station, her alarm woke her. She hopped out of bed, pulled on a fresh pair of jeans, a checked grey shirt and her grandmother's knitted cardigan, then headed outside with her camera.

Outside, she tiptoed down the steps at the front of the

cabin and into the copse of trees below. It wasn't dark but it wasn't light yet either, so everything felt slightly hazy – as if a thin invisible mist was winding its way through the town.

Finally at the river, she sat down on the rocky bank and waited. Soon, the sky began to lighten. The clouds around the tops of the mountains were clearing. The river became bluer and bluer, as if it was a painting and the artist was brushing in some extra splashes of colour. Then, the moment she'd been waiting for - the sun danced across the peaks of the mountains, giving each one a tiny orange crown before gliding into view.

Beth drank it in. Every second of it. The air, and the landscape, and the fact that she was hundreds of miles away from home, doing what she'd always promised her father she would do.

"I love you, Dad," she whispered, closing her eyes and clasping her necklace. "I wish we could have seen this together."

Entering the lobby, still dazzled by the beauty of the sunrise, Beth bumped almost straight into a coffee-wielding Blake.

"Hey," he was holding two travel mugs and handed her one. "I saw you head down to the river. Early start."

Beth sipped the coffee – Canadian coffee was *good* – and tugged at her oversized cardigan. "It was beautiful down there."

"Maybe I'll join you tomorrow?"

"Sure." They wandered towards the breakfast room and picked a table by the window. "So," she said, sitting down and wrapping both hands around the mug Blake had given her. "I looked at today's itinerary."

Blake's features crumpled into an amused frown. "You did?"

"I did. A car is picking us up..." she glanced at her phone for the time, "in exactly one hour's time for a trip to the infamous Alabama Glacier icefields."

Opposite her, Blake nearly spat out his coffee. "It's *A-tha-basca*," he said, almost coughing with laughter. "Not *Al-a-bama*, you donut."

"Donut?" Beth's cheeks were flushed, but she couldn't help laughing at herself. She raised her palms at him and shook her hair over her shoulder. "I'm not going to argue. I read the itinerary and still got it wrong. Clearly, I'm not cut out for this."

Blake, still chuckling, motioned for the waiter. Once again, he ordered pancakes with bacon and syrup and, ignoring the voice in her head that told her to ask for granola, she followed suit.

As they ate together, and chatted about the day ahead, she caught Blake smiling at her.

"You're not still laughing at me are you?"

"I was just admiring your outfit..."

Beth sat up and tugged at the sleeves of her cardigan. "Not very fashionable, I know. My grandmother knitted it..."

"I was talking about what's underneath the cardigan." Blake was looking straight at her and Beth felt herself visibly flinch.

"Underneath?"

As if he'd only just realised what he'd said, Blake clattered his fork loudly onto his plate and waved his hands at her. "I meant the shirt. Your shirt. Your checked shirt." He was speaking quickly and his neck was turning red around his collar line.

Beth looked down. Then remembered what she'd put on. A grey checked shirt. Almost identical to the ones she'd been making fun of Blake for wearing since they'd met in Vancouver.

As their eyes met, both of them started to laugh. And then, just as they'd managed to take a breath and were about to try and finish their breakfast, Emily appeared to tell them their cab was on the way.

"By the way," she said as she turned to go find her own table. "Love the coordinated looks today, guys." Then, with a playful nod, "Blake, did you lend Beth one of your shirts?"

As Emily walked away, Beth buried her head in her hands. She was laughing so hard that tears were springing to her eyes. And when she looked up, Blake's cheeks were wet too.

"Oh my goodness," she said, holding her side. "I don't remember the last time I laughed that hard."

Blake shook his head and placed his hands flat on the table. "Me neither."

The drive to the icefield was just a little over two hours. For the first part of the journey, the two of them looked out of their windows, listened to the cab driver's knowledgeable patter about Banff National Park and what they'd see up on the glacier. And then, eventually, Blake reached into his small day-pack and handed Beth a pile of handwritten notes.

"I thought you dictated all of your notes?" she quipped, taking the papers from him and starting to leaf through them.

"It's the feedback you asked for, on your blog."

Beth narrowed her eyes at him. "All this?" There must have been at least ten pages.

"I wanted to be thorough."

"Okay." Beth had expected a few tips, not an essay.

"You don't need to read it right now."

"No, no, I'm intrigued." She settled back into her seat and was aware of Blake watching her as she started to read.

The first page wasn't too bad – some compliments about her photography and her 'innate' ability to write compelling descriptions. But then, on page two, it turned into what Beth could only describe as an *assassination*. Blake had critiqued everything from her 'out-dated' web design and her 'clumsy' layout to her 'lack of theme, clarity, and direction'.

It was brutal.

And by the time she reached the end, her skin was burning with the effort of trying not to burst into tears.

Slowly, she put the notes down on the seat beside her.

Blake had finished with an enormously long list of 'next steps', including a complete redesign of the site, editing or removing eighty percent of her articles because they weren't 'SEO' friendly enough, and the suggestion to sit down and figure out what was actually *unique* about what she was doing because so far – he said –apart from a few stand-out pieces, she was just getting lost in the crowd. She was no different from the other thousands of bloggers writing mediocre material and trying to make it.

"What'd you think?" Blake was watching her expectantly.

"Thank you. I'll think about it." She couldn't say more than that because, if she did, she'd either cry or lose her temper.

For a moment, Blake didn't say anything. But then he tapped her arm and, looking a little concerned, said, "I didn't offend you did I?"

"No."

"I feel like I did."

Beth glanced at the driver, who was watching them in his rear-view mirror. "We can talk about it later."

Blake drummed his fingers on his thigh. His foot was twitching nervously up and down. "Come on, Greenwood. Don't take it personally. It's business."

Beth couldn't tell whether she was overreacting; he'd hit her where it hurt and she was too full of emotion to think clearly. So, she angled herself towards the window and tried to focus on what she needed to get out of the glacier trip in order to write a good article instead of the words 'mediocre' and 'lost in the crowd', hoping that her hurt pride would settle and she'd realise she was being a little too sensitive.

By the time they reached the icefields, however, any warmth she'd felt towards Blake O'Brien that morning had evaporated and, now, she could barely look at him.

Climbing out of the car, they were greeted by a tour guide who shepherded them towards a group of big-wheeled multicoloured ice-buses. They were provided with huge coats, hats, gloves and scarves and boarded their assigned bus without saying a word to one another.

The ice-buses, in a line of four, drove them from the visitor's centre right onto the glacier itself. Some chose to stay inside, not wanting to brave the cold, but Beth and Blake both disembarked.

"Woah, this is incredible." Blake was standing in the middle of the big white space beyond the buses, looking up at the mountain behind them.

Beth turned away. She just couldn't bring herself to be friendly towards him; whether he'd meant to or not, he'd managed to shatter her confidence. Made her question whether Harry was right. Whether she really was foolish to think she'd ever be able to achieve the kind of things her father had.

Shivering, she took some pictures of the tourists skidding about on the glacier, then headed back inside.

Back at the visitor's centre, Blake finally cornered her.

"Beth. Talk to me."

They were outside and the sun was shining, but the cold on the glacier had seeped into her bones and she wrapped her arms around herself. "Were they supposed to help?"

"My notes?"

"Mm hmm. Your notes. Were they supposed to help me? Or were you trying to destroy my self-esteem?"

Blake looked genuinely surprised. "I..."

"You tore me apart. My entire blog. My posts, the way the website looks... every single thing."

"Not everything. And I didn't tear it apart. I was trying to help. It's constructive criticism, that's all."

"There's nothing *constructive* about it. It's mean and cruel and I don't want to talk about it." Beth knew she sounded childish, but she didn't care.

"Come on, Greenwood..."

"No. I was stupid to ever think we could..."

"Could what?" Blake moved a little closer and put his hand on her forearm.

Beth shrugged him off and shook her head. "I was stupid to think we could be friends. This is a competition. If anything, we're enemies."

"Enemies? That's..."

But Beth was already walking away. "And *stop* calling me 'Greenwood'!"

Back at the B&B, Beth stayed in her room all evening. She didn't want to risk running into Blake, and she was panicking about the article that was due tomorrow. She'd submitted two so far: one about their first two days in Vancouver – Granville Island and Lynn Canyon – and one detailing their train trip through the Rockies. Both had been *okay*. But nothing spectacular. Certain that Blake's two pieces would have been far better than hers, she'd been avoiding looking at the Nomad website to see whether they'd gotten any good comments. But now, thinking of all the things he'd said in his 'constructive criticism' she figured that she might as well find out what other people thought.

The World Travel Finalists' Tour was prominently featured on Nomad's home page. There was the video of her and Blake, and then links to an interactive map of their trip and the articles they were submitting.

Blake's first was, surprisingly, not about the artists they'd met on Granville Island or their experience at the suspension bridge in Lynn Canyon Park; it was a listicle. *Top ten tourist spots around Vancouver*.

His second article was similar: *Five Excellent Reasons to Travel Gold Leaf on the Rocky Mountaineer*.

He was writing exactly the same kind of material he wrote on his blog. The kind that would generate traffic for Nomad's website. Scrolling through the comments that readers had made, almost all were positive. *Great tips. Good job, Blake. Rooting for you, Blake.*

Beth's stomach twitched and her skin prickled with anxiety.

She clicked through to her own articles. They were the polar opposite of Blake's. She'd written about what *she* had experienced. She'd written about Todd the student, who was saving up for college, and about the artists they'd met. She'd written about the super-friendly Canadian lady who had, without question, shown Beth the way to her favourite coffee house. She'd written about swimming in the freezing cold waters in Lynn Canyon Park, and about Doris and Mike and how brave they were to go on a single travellers' trip at the ages of eight-five and ninety.

As she navigated to the comments section below her most recent piece, her stomach clenched nervously. She didn't have as many comments as Blake, but they were more detailed, and definitely more effusive.

Such a refreshing style, amazing to read. Can't wait to see more from this exciting new writer. Charles Greenwood's daughter has clearly inherited his talent...

And suddenly, as she looked back at what she'd written, she realised that Blake was right. But not in the way he thought he was.

Yes, she probably did need to be more search engine friendly. And, no, her articles weren't optimised for key words or designed to be click-bait for would-be travellers.

But they were *authentic*.

In his ten-page critique, Blake had mentioned - as a negative - that Beth's articles sounded more like excerpts from a travel journal than articles on a commercial blog.

But maybe that was precisely the point.

Maybe that's what she'd been struggling with all this time. Maybe she didn't want to be commercial. Just like she didn't want to settle down in Oxford and work at Cooper's and marry Harry, she didn't want to sanitise her blog. She didn't want to make it all about clicks and traffic. She wanted it to be about *her* and her experience of the world.

So, instead of writing down the ten best reasons to visit the Athabasca Glacier, Beth wrote from her heart. She wrote about the alarming rate at which the icefields were melting, and the irony of the tourists who marvel at it but who don't seem to care that, very soon, it might not be there anymore.

When she finally stopped writing and went to bed, she felt calm. And she knew precisely what she was going to say to Blake O'Brien first thing tomorrow morning.

CHAPTER TWELVE

Day Six, Banff and Jasper

She found Blake down by the river, in the exact spot she'd watched the sunrise the day before. He was wearing a dark grey hoodie and had his knees tucked up under his chin. As she sat down beside him, she handed him a flask of coffee.

"Morning O'Brien... peace offering."

Blake took the flask and balanced it on the rocks in front of him. "Beth," he said, turning so that he was facing her. "I'm so sorry if I offended you. *Nothing* I said about your blog was personal. I had my business-hat on. I was just trying to help."

"I know." She met his eyes and smiled a little. "I guess you just hit a nerve. Several nerves, actually."

"I really am sorry..."

"You don't need to apologise. I should have been more mature about it." She sighed and slurped luke-warm coffee from her flask. "For a long time, Harry's been telling me I should give up writing. So, I guess the things you said made me wonder if he was right."

"Beth, there's no way you should give up writing. Are you crazy?"

"Don't worry. I'm not going to. Actually, I think, in a weird way, you might have helped me."

Blake frowned, clearly surprised.

"Last night, I thought really hard about what makes my blog different. How I can make it stand out."

"That's great." Blake sat up a little straighter and unfolded his knees.

"In your *critique* you said my articles are too much like journal entries..."

Blake's neck flushed pink. "I..."

"It's fine." Beth waved dismissively. "Because I realised that's exactly what I *want* my blog to be like. I know it's not very commercial. And maybe those kinds of articles won't win me the competition. Maybe they won't draw in hundreds of new customers for Nomad. But they're the kind of articles I'll be *proud* to write. The kind of articles I'd have been proud to show my dad." She sat back and breathed in a slow deliberate breath. "So, that's what I'm going to write. And if it means I don't make it as a 'successful' blogger. Then..." she shrugged. "Then I guess that's okay."

After breakfast, Emily appeared for their usual morning briefing and told them they'd be heading for the small alpine town of Jasper, where she'd booked them on the two p.m. Skytram up to The Whistlers mountain.

"Skytram? So that's like... a cable car?" Beth's stomach lurched at the thought of it.

"Sure is. The longest aerial tramway in Canada." Emily smiled. "It's like a little glass pod that takes you up over the trees to this amazing viewing point on the mountain. It's really spectacular. I was worried it would be closed today as they'd warned about wind, but I called ahead and it's fine. Your slot is at two, so we better get moving. It's a three and a half hour drive and I'm sure you'll want to make a couple of stops on the way to take in the scenery."

Beth absent-mindedly scratched her fingernails against the grain of the wooden table. Swallowing hard, she asked, "This aerial tram... how high does it go exactly?"

"Oh pretty high. It dangles right above–" Emily stopped mid-sentence because Blake was shaking his head at her. "Oh, Beth. Are you scared of heights?"

"I'll be fine."

"Are you sure? I could always call the office and see if they'd be happy for Blake to do it alone?"

"No. I want to do it. I'll be fine."

And Beth kept telling herself that she'd be fine.

As she packed her suitcase. As she climbed into the back

of a large people-carrier taxi cab with Blake. As she listened to Emily chatter excitedly to the driver about the beauty of Canada's national parks.

Even as they reached the Skytram's starting point and she read the sign that said it would be taking them two-thousand metres above sea-level, she told herself it would all be *okay* once she was up there.

But as they climbed into their little glass pod, and as the pod was slowly guided – on thick metal wires – up into the air, she started to tremble.

At first, it wasn't particularly high and the treetops below gave the illusion of safety. But when they reached the point where they were way above even the tops of the trees, Beth started to feel woozy.

With a pod all to themselves, Blake was watching her. "Are you okay, Greenwood?"

"I'm fine."

"You look like you might vomit."

"No. I'm fine."

Blake nodded. "Okay." But then, just as he turned to take a video of their journey, something made a loud creaking sound and the pod swayed from side to side.

A small *eeep* escaped Beth's lips. She wanted to get up and leap across to sit beside Blake, but she couldn't move.

"We've stopped. Why have we stopped?"

A voice over the tannoy announced, "Ladies and Gentlemen, we're experiencing some technical difficulties. We'll have you moving again any minute now. Just sit tight."

"As if we could go anywhere else?!" Beth exclaimed nervously.

Holding up his hands as if Beth was a frightened rabbit, Blake stood up and moved over to sit beside her.

"It's going to be okay. We'll get moving any minute. And we're nearly at the top."

Beth accidentally looked down at the long-long way between them and the ground, and groaned. "Talk to me about something." She nudged closer to Blake's side and tried to focus on his face, his hands, his eyes... anything but the overwhelming sensation that they were about to drop to their deaths.

"Okay. What kind of something?"

"Anything. Your parents. What are they like?"

"My parents?"

"Yeah. Mr and Mrs O'Brien." Beth motioned for him to hurry up.

"Um. Okay. So, my mom's a school teacher and my dad's an engineer. They're pretty great. Married young but always stuck together, made it work, you know. Very supportive." Blake rubbed his neck a little sheepishly. "Actually, if it wasn't for them I wouldn't have got as far as I have with my blog. They paid my rent for the first three months after I quit my job."

"Wow. That's generous."

"I had a business plan, showed them exactly how I was planning on starting to bring in income within six months. But, really, I had no idea if it would work." Blake wrinkled his nose slightly. "I'm glad it did. I'm glad I didn't have to rely on them for too long."

Beth nodded, trying to picture what Mr and Mrs O'Brien would look like. She was about to ask him to show her a photo when the cable car made a sudden, vicious, jolt. Beth shrieked and grabbed hold of Blake's arm. Her heart was thundering in her chest. Her head was swimming and her hands felt clammy.

"Hey, it's okay. It's just the wind. We'll get moving any second." Blake's voice was soft and gentle. Slowly, he wrapped his arm around her and pulled her a little closer. "I got you."

Concentrating on the warmth of his body against hers, Beth leaned into him and closed her eyes. "My parents met young too."

"They did?" If Blake was surprised that she'd started to talk about her family, he didn't show it.

"Straight out of college. Funny really. They were so different. Mum hated travelling. Dad lived for it. But they managed to stay totally in love."

"Your mum hates travel?"

Beth nodded, and nudged a little closer. "She loves her home. Her things around her. And she's pretty terrified of flying."

"So she never went places with your dad?"

"Nope. He sent her these super romantic postcards and letters though, every place he went." She sighed and looked down at her fingernails. "I guess that's why I tried so hard to make it work with Harry. I thought we could be like them. But it turns out he's not very keen on the idea of a wife who goes off gallivanting around the world. And I'm not very keen on staying put."

Beth looked quickly up at Blake then sat up a little straighter. "We broke up. Harry and I. At least, I think we did. He said he needed me to choose between this..." she waved her hand at their surroundings. "And settling down."

"And you chose this?" Blake's deep brown eyes were fixed on hers and, not for the first time, she tried not to count the flecks of green in them.

"I did."

"You know, settling down doesn't have to mean staying in one place." Blake was speaking so quietly that his words were almost lost in the air between them.

"It doesn't?"

"Well, I've always wanted to find someone to be away *with* – if that makes sense."

"You mean someone to travel with?"

"Exactly. To me, marriage is about finding your missing piece. The one person whose dreams fit with yours. Who makes you feel like anything is possible." He shrugged a little and Beth wasn't sure if it was the cold making his cheeks blush, or the fact that he'd been so open with her. "That's what I think, anyway."

"I didn't know you were interested in *the one* – I figured you'd want to stay footloose and carefree. Travelling solo. Doing whatever you want."

"Then maybe you don't know me well enough yet." Blake's voice had melted into something soft and warm. His eyes moved to Beth's freckled cheeks, and then to her lips.

She moved a little closer, suddenly completely unfazed by the huge chasm of empty space below them. Blake pressed his forehead gently against hers and stroked the back of her neck.

She could feel his lips, so close to hers they were almost touching.

And then...

The cable car lurched and with a loud *crank* and a *clunk* started moving.

Beth sat back. Blake smiled coyly and glanced behind them. "They couldn't have waited thirty more seconds...?"

Beth smiled back and bit her lower lip to stop it spreading into a grin. And as Blake shuffled and started to take back his arm, she reached up to stop him. "Just until we reach the other side," she said.

He nodded. "Just until we reach the other side."

That evening, they sat together in their Jasper B&B's small cosy lounge to work on their articles. Despite being sunny during the day, at night the temperature in Jasper dropped to almost-freezing, so the warmth of the fire and its delicate orange glow made it feel more like winter than spring.

Beside her, Blake was typing quickly on his laptop. But,

despite the typewriter-sounds app he'd downloaded for her, Beth was still struggling.

Sighing and flipping her iPad case closed, she leaned back and put her hands behind her head, jutting out her elbows and enjoying the stretch.

"It's still not the same, I'm afraid," she said, taking out her earphones.

"Missing your typewriter?"

Beth nodded.

"Well, not long now until you're reunited. Only... eight days."

"Gosh. Are we a week into the competition already?"

"We are."

Beth breathed out slowly, trying to ignore the tugging sense of disappointment in her chest. Was she disappointed that the trip would soon end? Or disappointed because she'd just realised that the thought of anything more than a friendship between her and Blake was foolish. They'd barely known each other a week. In eight more days, one of them would win the competition and be whisked off on a one-in-a-lifetime journey. And the other would go back home to their normal life.

As if he could read her mind, Blake closed the lid of his laptop and turned to face her. His arm was resting on the back of the couch. She wanted to lean into him, the way she had in the cable car, but she didn't.

"Beth. Earlier. When we..."

She felt herself starting to blush, and hoped he'd assume it was the warmth of the fire. "You mean when we almost..."

Blake nodded. "I feel like we should talk about it. I wasn't expecting it. I mean... I kind of thought you hated me."

Beth tucked her hair behind her ear. "Honestly? So did I." She nudged him playfully. "Maybe we were just caught up in the moment."

"Maybe." Blake's hand was near her shoulder and his fingers were almost touching her. He reached up and brushed his index finger against the small soft piece of skin just below her ear. It sent a tingle down her spine.

"I suppose it's silly. Us being..." she trailed off. She didn't know how to finish.

"We're competitors." Blake said. "One of us is going to *win* this thing and go travelling around the world for a year."

"Plus my home is in England and yours is in Toronto."

"Right." Blake sat up and slowly took his hand away. "So, we should just be..."

"Friends?" Even as she said it, Beth realised she wanted Blake to stop talking and kiss her. But he didn't. He just nodded slowly and said, "Yes. Friends. Exactly."

CHAPTER THIRTEEN

Day Seven, Jasper

So far, in the first week of their Canada trip, they'd been offered just a few un-timetabled hours here and there to 'relax'. Mostly, because that time was limited, they'd spent it working on their articles but with nothing due until tomorrow, Beth finally allowed herself a lie-in.

She stayed in her big comfy bed until nine-thirty, by which time breakfast downstairs was over, so she ventured out to find somewhere to eat.

She hadn't asked Blake what he'd got planned for the day, although she had found herself looking for him in the lounge before she left and mentally kicking herself for being disappointed he wasn't there.

Wandering out onto Jasper's main street, Beth looked up

at the mountains. How was she ever going to get used to not seeing this kind of beauty every day when she got home?

Taking her camera, she decided that today would be a day for photos. Walking, and observing, and taking pictures.

She'd called her mum last night, and had spoken to Jo several times via text, but hadn't spoken to Harry since their phone call back when she was in Vancouver. Stopping outside a coffee shop with big windows and comfortable looking chairs, she looked at her phone. It would be mid-afternoon in Oxford. She could call Harry, check in. After yesterday, and her near-kiss with Blake, she was feeling strangely guilty. Even though she was pretty sure things between her and Harry were over. Even though *not* being his girlfriend anymore filled her with an overwhelming sense of relief. She still felt as if she shouldn't be feeling attracted to someone else so soon.

Especially not Blake O'Brien.

But then, perhaps she wasn't attracted to him at all. Perhaps she was confused. It was good that she and Blake had decided just to be friends.

Much better.

Just as she had decided this, and resolved to stop thinking about Blake's deep Canadian accent and mesmerising eyes, as if fate was taunting her, he appeared on the other side of the coffee shop window.

Settling into a brown leather armchair, he looked up, saw Beth outside and waved. "Come join me," he mouthed, pointing at his coffee, smiling, and rubbing his belly to indicate that it was good and she'd be missing out if she didn't.

Adjusting her camera on her shoulder, she inhaled through her nose and breathed slowly out through her mouth. Then she went inside.

"Fancy seeing you here," Blake said with a smile as she said down beside him. "Have I ever told you how impressive that camera of yours is?"

Beth glanced at it, then self-consciously removed the cap and started wiping the lens with the end of her sleeve. "Thanks."

"Photography's definitely a strong point of yours."

It was a genuine compliment, but Beth couldn't help teasing him. "Mmm. I believe you briefly mentioned it in your *critique...*"

Blake tapped a finger on the side of his coffee cup. "Well, there you go then. You're ace."

"Ace?"

"You Brits don't say 'ace'?"

"No. We use proper English."

"Oh, well, I'm glad we're back to our traditional style of competitive banter."

Beth stood up and started to walk over to the counter. "You had breakfast? I'm getting a muffin I think."

"Sure. I'll have one."

When she returned, Blake wolfed his down in just a couple of mouthfuls, brushed the crumbs from his chin, and said, "So, today, what's the plan?"

"Well, *my* plan is to just enjoy this beautiful town. Take some photos. Enjoy the fact I'm not dangling thousands of metres above the ground."

"Want company?"

Beth put down her now-empty coffee cup and brushed her hands on her jeans. She should say no. She should do her own thing, let Blake do his, and go back to finding him annoying and arrogant. But, despite herself, she said, "Okay."

After wandering up and down Jasper's main streets for a couple of hours, Blake suggested they get take out sandwiches and go somewhere off the beaten track.

"I read about a great picnic spot," he said, taking out his phone and showing Beth a TripAdvisor page.

She agreed and after purchasing food, getting lost a couple of times, and having to eventually stop for directions because Google Maps wasn't helping, they arrived at a small wooden bridge and a startlingly blue, slow-moving river.

"It's a bridge, but a very very small one," Blake said, settling down on a nearby bit of river bank.

"I think I can handle it." Beth put down her bag and raised her camera. "Hold that pose." Blake was looking at the river, sitting with one knee bent and his arm resting casually on top of it. He turned to look at her. "No, no. Look that way." She pointed to the water, then snap-snap-snap took three images in quick succession.

"You think I've got a back-up career as a male-model if this doesn't work out?" Blake asked, trying to sound cocky but clearly more self-conscious than he wanted her to realise.

"Don't quit the day job just yet." Beth sat down and showed him the pictures. "They're good though. I can send them to you if you like, for your article?" As she said it, she instantly regretted it. Good imagery was the *one* thing she had that Blake didn't. But thankfully, he shook his head.

"It's okay. I'll go with a good old selfie." He held up his phone and motioned for Beth to lean in. "Say cheese, Greenwood."

Beth frowned at him, but smiled at the camera and stuck out her tongue. Then... "Blake. Wait."

"You look fine..."

"No," she reached up and held his hand in place. "Behind us."

Blake shifted the phone, squinted at it, then his eyes widened. "What do we do?" he whispered.

"I have no idea," Beth hissed at him. "We don't have *bears* in Oxford. You're the Canadian. Don't they teach you this stuff in school?"

"Not in Toronto!"

Beth slowly started to turn around, gripping her camera so tightly that her knuckles were turning white. "Oh my goodness, Blake. It's a mother and a baby."

Blake turned around too and grabbed Beth's arm. "Beth, that's not good. Mother bears are *super protective*."

"Okay, okay, I read about this. They had a leaflet in the

B&B. Bears don't really like humans. She won't attack us for no reason, so let's just stay put and keep still and she'll probably move right by us."

"Or..." Blake glanced back at the bridge. "We could run."

"I don't think we should run."

"I'm pretty sure it's grizzlies you don't run from. Black bears are fine. They won't chase us. Come on, leave the food, let's go."

"A minute ago, you didn't know anything about bears and now you're an expert?" Beth could feel her voice rising in volume, so she lowered it to a whisper and shook her head. "You run if you like, I'm staying put." She turned and sat, very still, facing the bears. Lifting her camera, she gently clicked some pictures. Then, slowly, the mother bear and her cub started to move away into the trees.

"They're going," whispered Blake, visibly relaxing.

Beth's heart was pounding in her chest. Grinning, she turned to Blake and impulsively hugged him. "I can't believe I just saw a bear up close. Two bears!" She waved her camera at him.

"Let's see..." Blake looked over her shoulder as she scrolled through the images she'd taken. "Beth, these are stunning."

"Did you get any?" Beth gestured to Blake's phone.

"Ah. No. I was too busy protecting us to worry about taking photos."

"Protecting us? You wanted to run."

"For safety."

Beth laughed, shaking her head at him. And as they got up and started to walk back towards town, she said, "Do you want me to tell everyone you were super-brave?"

"Yes," he said. "Yes, I do."

On the outskirts of town, Blake said he needed to go grab a few 'supplies', so Beth headed back to the B&B on her own. Almost as soon as she was back in her room, she downloaded the images of the bears. Now, if only she could get over her lack-of-typewriter and write something spectacular about them. Something that would blow Blake's articles out of the water.

She was editing a couple of pictures into black and white when there was a knock at her door. When she opened it, there was no-one there. Just a small white box sitting on the floor.

She picked it up. On top, there was an envelope and a card inside that read:

I hope this helps the inspiration flow. Your friend, Bear-Hunter Extraordinaire, Blake x

Beth sat down on the edge of the bed and slowly opened the box. Inside, sat a brand new, shiny, miniature version of what looked like a typewriter. Beside it was an instruction leaflet and, as soon as she picked it up, she knew what it was for.

"A typewriter for my iPad," she breathed, tears springing to her eyes.

Immediately, she set it down on the small round table in the corner of the room and slotted her iPad into the holder at the back. Opening a Word document, she typed *h-e-l-l-o* and there it was; the sound and the feel of her typewriter. Right there, beneath her fingers.

Straight away, she started typing. And she typed, and typed, and typed. Until there were no more words left inside her.

The next morning, she found Blake standing outside on the veranda, looking up at the mountains. Without saying anything, she walked right up to him and hugged him. For a moment, he stood stiff as a statue, but then he let his arms fold around her.

"You liked the gift then?"

Beth stood back and wrapped her cardigan a little tighter around her middle. "Where did you find it? I mean... here?" She tilted her head towards the town's main street. "I can't imagine they've got many tech shops in Jasper."

Blake leaned on the railing of the veranda and bit his lower lip, looking at her as if he wasn't sure whether he should tell her or not.

Beth raised her right eyebrow at him.

"I ordered it back when we were in Kamloops. Asked for it to be delivered here."

"Seriously?" She was still hugging herself against the crisp early-morning air, but her skin suddenly felt warmer and the sensation spread from her chest, up her neck, to her cheeks. "Why would you do that?"

A coy smile fleetingly crossed Blake's lips and he looked away. "I wanted to help. That's all."

"Well," Beth stepped up beside him and nudged his ribs with her upper arm. "It did."

"Yeah?"

"So much." She met his eyes and blinked slowly. "Thank you, Blake."

"You're very welcome... *friend*." Blake's smile spread into his usual cheeky grin. "See how good we are at this?"

"At being friends?"

"Mm hmm."

"Oh yeah, we're smashing it." Beth laughed and punched him lightly on the arm. "Come on then, *friend,* let's go eat. Our cab will be here soon."

Heading back inside, Blake turned and looked at the mountains behind them. "I'll be kind of sad to leave this part of Canada."

"Me too. And I'm not sure how I feel about being cooped up in a train with you for four whole days."

"Oh, come on, it's a dream come true."

Beth shook her head and stepped past him. "We'll see."

CHAPTER FOURTEEN

Day Eight - Jasper to Edmonton

The train they boarded in Jasper was very different to the luxury *Rocky Mountaineer* that had taken them from Vancouver to Banff.

This train was, aptly, called *The Canadian* and it was a large shiny sleeper-train that would carry them hundreds of miles from Alberta, across the Saskatchewan plains, to Ontario – Blake's home-county. They'd finish their journey in six days' time in Toronto, with a visit to Niagara Falls.

Six days, and it would all be over. Six days. Three more articles to write. And then either she or Blake would be crowned the winner of the competition.

So far, it had been nothing short of a rollercoaster; she had started the trip almost certain she wouldn't win, intending to simply enjoy the vacation. Then she'd met Blake and her competitive streak had fired into action, only to be torn to pieces when he offered his constructive criticism of her blog. She had spent several hours feeling like a failure, wondering why Nomad had picked her and whether she was letting down her father's memory, her friends, or herself by not being good enough.

And then she'd had her epiphany; the ray of light which had made her realise that her strength was in her depth of feeling and the way she expressed it with her writing, in her photographs and the moments they captured, and in the fact that she didn't want to change herself just to fit a 'commercial' mould.

In that moment, she'd decided that what she needed from the competition was to finish it feeling as if she'd been true to herself. If she managed that, she would go home feeling proud of herself.

And so, she boarded *The Canadian* with the resolution to soak up every last second of the next six days, to write from her heart, and to let fate decide whether she was destined to win or not.

She would try her best, be herself, and whatever was meant to happen would happen.

And as for Blake O'Brien? Well, she would quite simply forget about their moment in the cable car. She'd forget how it had felt when he'd had his arm around her, and when his lips had almost brushed against hers. She'd stop thinking about his magical eyes and his Hollywood dimples. And she would focus on being his friend.

And if that failed, she'd remind herself that he really had been a jerk for ninety percent of the beginning of their trip, and hopefully that would be enough to make the fluttering in her stomach go away.

Because, really, there could never be anything more than friendship between them, could there?

They lived on different sides of the world, she'd only just broken up with Harry and was probably still in shock, and whoever won the competition would soon be in possession of a round-the-world plane ticket.

Even friendship was a stretch under those circumstances.

Pen-pals, or email-pals, would probably be as much as they'd manage.

"Hey Greenwood, get a move on..." Blake nudged her. She'd stopped in the middle of the platform and was causing a traffic-jam.

"Sorry," she muttered. "Is this us?"

Blake checked the cabin number on their ticket. "Sure is. We got sleeper cabins, how cool is that?"

Beth frowned. "Aren't they all sleeper cabins? It's a four-day trip."

Blake chuckled. "You might as well *burn* your itinerary, you know."

"I like things to be..."

"A surprise. I know. But there's such a thing as being chronically underprepared."

Beth tutted and stepped up into the train.

Walking down the inside of a carriage lined with

windows on one side and doors on the other, Blake gestured to them and said, "These are cabins. So, we get an actual door and a washroom. But back there…" He pointed to the carriage behind them. "They've got open bunks with curtains they can pull across at night. And behind that, there's just ordinary seats… like airplane seats."

"People do a four-day journey like that?"

"Yep."

Beth inhaled quickly. "Well, I'm very glad we've got beds. And doors."

"Me too. And you don't mind bunking in with me for three nights, do you?"

Beth stopped and looked over her shoulder. Blake had come to a halt outside one of the cabin doors. "With you?" A fierce heat bubbled across her skin and up into her cheeks. "That can't be... let me see your ticket." She took it from him and held it next to hers, then breathed a sigh of relief, looked up, and punched him lightly on the arm. "You're an idiot, you know that?"

Blake's face had reddened. He was trying not to laugh. "Sorry. I couldn't resist. Don't worry Greenwood, we're neighbours not roommates." He reached over and tapped the door to the left of his. "That one's yours, I think."

Beth handed him back his ticket and took the key she'd been given at arrivals from her pocket. Inside her cabin there was barely enough room to turn around. Folded down from the wall, there was a small single bed. Opposite the door, a square window that looked out onto the station platform. And opposite the bed, a minuscule en-suite bathroom. Beth reached out her arms; she could touch each side of the cabin with the tips of her fingers and, suddenly, she understood why Emily had made them check in their cases and take just hand luggage for the train trip.

"Knock knock!" Emily's chirpy voice accompanied a swift tapping on the door as she pushed it open. "Wow, this is adorable." She shuffled inside and peeked at the en-suite. "But this is goodbye for now."

"I can't believe you're not coming with us."

Emily smiled thinly. "I know. What can I say? It's cheaper – and quicker, I guess – for me to get a six-hour train to Calgary and then *fly* to Toronto. This way," she said, not trying to disguise her bitterness, "they get me back in the office a whole three-days quicker."

"But who will remind us what we're actually supposed to be doing?"

Emily laughed a little. "I think you'll manage – this next bit is pretty simple. Just stay on the train until it reaches Toronto. You can get off for some air at Edmonton or Winnipeg, but other than that it goes straight through. And I'll be waiting for you at the other end."

Outside on the platform, an extra-loud whistle sounded and Emily stepped back out into the corridor. "Got to go!" She waved, shouted goodbye to Blake as she passed his cabin, and then she was gone.

Beth sat down on her small fold-out bed and watched as the train pulled out of the station. She felt nervous and she wasn't sure why, but she'd barely had time to contemplate it before Blake put his head around the door and said, "Want to find the lounge car? I need coffee and good scenery. I'm missing those mountains already."

For the rest of the morning, Beth felt as if they did nothing but eat snacks, drink coffee, and talk. *The Canadian*'s lounge car was like any other train car, but bigger. It had huge windows on either side, a mixture of leather bench-seats with tables, and comfy recliner chairs.

Beth and Blake settled themselves at a table and barely moved until the lunch bell rang.

Beth glanced at her watch. "Darn, I was going to get changed before we ate."

"It's not a cruise ship, I don't think black-tie is necessary."

Beth raised her right eyebrow at him. "I was just going to swap my baggy cardigan for something a little nicer. I wasn't thinking of going full-on ball gown."

"You look great just as you are."

Beth looked down at her fingernails and tried to shrug off the compliment.

Friendly. Blake was just being friendly.

"By the way," he said as they got up and started to walk towards the dining car. "How do you do that with your eyebrow?"

As she looked at him, she noticed he was trying – and failing – to mimic her. But instead of moving just one eyebrow, he was tweaking both up in a comical arch that made his forehead wrinkle and his hairline twitch.

"Years of practice. You'll never manage it."

As they sat down, Blake tutted. "Yet another thing you're better at, Greenwood."

"I'd say the *only* thing. Your articles are blowing mine out of the water. I've seen the comments they're getting. At least ten times the amount mine are."

Blake picked up a menu, not looking at her as he replied, "Yeah, but your comments are *deep*."

"What do you mean?"

He put down his menu and took out his phone, navigating to Beth's icefields article. "Look. You're getting people write entire *paragraphs* on how much they love what you've written. My comments are one-liners. *Yay, go Blake... Great job, Blake...* In fact, I wouldn't be surprised if most of mine were written by my buddy Karl under a pseudonym."

"Karl?" Beth chuckled. "Is he your bestie?"

"The best of a bad bunch," Blake quipped, then tilted his head and looked a little more serious. "Nah. I'm kidding. My buddies are great. Karl and I have known each other since we were at school. He's bagged my 'friends and family' ticket if I win this thing."

"Oh, wow. So, you've thought about who you'll take?"

"Haven't you?"

Beth shifted a little in her seat and nibbled the inside of

her cheek. "I guess, Jo? We worked together at Cooper's. But then... I don't know. I love her but she's a bit of a party animal and I'm most definitely *not*."

"And I guess things between you and Henry..." Blake cleared his throat and picked up his menu again. "Harry," Beth corrected. "Things between *Harry* and I are finished."

"You don't think he'd change his mind about going travelling if you won?"

Beth looked out of the window. For some reason, looking at Blake was making her stomach feel jittery. "No. Definitely not. He's been offered a promotion at Cooper's. They're opening a new branch. There's no way he'd give that up."

"Even for you?" Blake was looking at her intently; she could feel it.

"Especially not for me." She finally made herself look at Blake and, as her eyes met his, the jittering spread from her stomach to her chest. "He told me to take some time to think about things, but I've known for a long time that we weren't right for each other. I guess it just took this trip to make me realise it..." She sighed a little and realised she was speaking quietly. "If I'm honest, we've been drifting apart for a long time. It's just that neither of us wanted to admit it. He's not..." She trailed off, then breathed in sharply and forced herself to look away. "He's not going to be my plus one."

"So then, your mom?"

Beth laughed a little. "She likes her home and her job and her friends too much to leave for a year... maybe I'll have to just travel solo. Or maybe you'll beat me, hands down, and I won't have to worry about it."

"Well," Blake waved for the waiter who was moving through the car taking orders. "On the off chance that you do manage to kick my butt and win this thing, you could always..."

"Are you ready to order, Sir?" The waiter cut Blake's sentence short and Beth realised she was holding her breath. What had he been about to say? She could always... stay home? Give him her ticket? Take him with her?

CHAPTER FIFTEEN

*A*fter lunch, they were standing on the train's outside viewing platform – a small space at the very end of the train that allowed them to feel the wind on their faces as they watched the scenery rushing past – waiting for the approach to Edmonton to begin, when Blake grabbed Beth's arm and pointed into the cabin. "Hey, is that Doris?"

"It is!" Beth waved through the window. "And Mike..." She frowned, unsure if she was imagining things, then looked at Blake. "Did they just?"

"He kissed her on the cheek..."

"They're smiling at each other. She said he was boring and that she couldn't stand sitting next to him!"

"Well, it looks like Mike brought his A-game and won her round." Blake opened the door and stepped back into the carriage, striding over and giving Doris a welcoming embrace before shaking Mike's hand.

Beth joined them and, leaning close to Doris's ear, whispered, "Doris, are you and Mike...?"

Doris looked at her. Her bright blue eyes were sparkling, and she giggled like a schoolgirl. "Sit down, dear, and I'll tell you all about it."

So, Beth, Mike, Doris, and Blake squeezed onto bench-seats opposite one another. Doris and Mike were holding hands. Beth and Blake exchanged a quizzical glance.

"Did I miss something?" Blake asked playfully. "I thought you two were *solo* travellers."

"Oh, we were," Doris replied, smiling at Mike. "And at first I thought he was a terrible bore."

"And I thought she talked too much," added Mike, slowly.

"But then we ended up having dinner together at Lake Louise..."

"There was only one free table in the restaurant..."

"And the view was just beautiful. I was lost for words..." Doris chuckled at herself.

"So, I finally got a word in edgeways..."

"And we just..."

"Hit it off," they said in unison.

Beth found herself grinning. Her chest felt warm and tingly. Seeing the two of them, finishing each other's sentences and looking at each another as if they'd discovered something wonderful, made her feel utterly joyful.

"Well, who would have thought?" Blake tapped the table triumphantly.

"Certainly not us," laughed Doris. She glanced at Mike. "Should I tell them?"

Mike pursed his lips thoughtfully, then slowly said, "Yes. I think so."

"Well... we decided to get married." Doris's lips spread into a grin that lightened her entire face.

"Married?" Beth felt her mouth drop open a little.

"Indeed," replied Mike.

"But you've only known each other..." Blake was counting on his fingers. "Six days?"

"Young man," tutted Mike. "When you're ninety years old, six days might as well be six years. I've been alone for too long, and I thought to myself – *Mike... are you going to let this wonderful woman slip out of your grasp, or for once in your life are you going to be brave enough to ask for what you want?*"

Doris squeezed Mike's hand and leaned into his shoulder. "And when he asked me, I thought – *Doris, you've never taken a risk in your life. It's time to do something crazy. So, I said yes.*"

Suddenly, Blake stood up and clapped his hands together. "This is fantastic!" He looked genuinely excited. "The most amazing thing I've ever heard. Wait right there... I'm going to find us some champagne. This deserves a celebration."

Doris reached up and patted Blake's arm. "That's very sweet of you my darling boy, but perhaps we should wait until after the wedding for the celebrations?"

"Ah, but we won't be at the wedding to celebrate, Doris. Let me treat you..."

"Actually, you *could* be at the wedding." Mike looked questioningly at Doris and she nodded excitedly. "You see, I've got a friend in Winnipeg who's a minister and I gave him a call."

"He's going to marry us when we stop there. In two days' time." Doris reached out to take Beth's hand. "Would the two of you like to be our witnesses?"

Beth felt tears spring to her eyes. She looked at Blake, who nudged her gently in the ribs, then back at Doris. "Of course, we'll be your witnesses. Of course."

"And perhaps, Beth," said Doris tentatively, "you'd be kind enough to help me find an outfit when we stop at Edmonton? All of my smart clothes are in my case and they won't let me take it out of the hold until we reach Toronto."

"Of course I will. We don't have long though; I think the stop over is only an hour?"

"I'm not fussy. Just something smart with a splash of colour," smiled Doris.

"Okay," said Beth, looking up at the clock above the door. "Then I'll go grab my things. We should be at Edmonton any minute now."

An hour later, Doris and Beth were standing in a small clothes boutique near Edmonton station trying on hats.

"I feel like a hat is too much," said Doris, putting back the wide-brimmed navy blue one she'd had in her hand. "I'd like to wear my hair down, but I feel it's a bit silly at my age. My daughter is always telling me to cut it, but I've had long hair since I was a girl. It wouldn't feel like me."

Beth reached up and touched the neat little bun that Doris had pinned in place at the nape of her neck. "You absolutely should wear it down."

"You think so?"

Beth nodded. "I'll help you get ready. You're going to look *beautiful* Doris."

Doris batted her hand playfully at Beth and pursed her lips. "Oh, get away with you."

"What will your daughter think about all this?" Beth asked as they started making their way back to the train.

"Oh, she'll be furious. But I don't particularly care. She's always been a little... rigid." Doris tutted and smiled affectionately. "I love her. But she's not one for spontaneity. Mind you, until now, I haven't been either."

Beth bit her lower lip thoughtfully, then said, "Doris, how do you *know* that this is the right thing? I mean, six days?"

"Honestly? I don't. But I know I want to figure it out. I know I don't want this trip to end and for us to never see each other again."

"Where do you both live? What will you do when you get home?"

"Well... we both live in Toronto. Opposite sides of the city but not too far. We'll keep our own houses for now.

Maybe we'll take it in turns to stay with one another. Maybe we'll sell up and buy somewhere new with a view of a lake and a big old veranda and rocking chairs and a porch swing." Doris smiled wistfully. "I don't know what we'll do. And, to be honest with you, that's what makes it so exciting. All my life, I've wanted to know what's next. I've wanted to plan and prepare and organise everyone. But Mike's so calm and laid back. He makes me feel like it's okay to just... see what happens."

"It's wonderful that you found one another." Beth paused as they approached the train station steps and looped Doris's arm through hers.

"It is," replied Doris. "Perhaps you'll be next?"

Beth shook her head, concentrating on helping Doris navigate the stairs. "Oh, I'm not sure about that."

At the top, Blake and Mike were waiting for them. Mike reached out to take Doris's arm and her shopping bags, and Blake almost did the same but stopped himself midway. Instead, he lingered awkwardly with his arms by his sides.

"Success on the outfit-front?" he asked casually.

"I'd say so," Beth replied. "What are you going to wear?"

"Oh, I'm sure I've got something I can spruce up for the occasion."

"Not another of your fabled checked shirts?"

"Just you wait and see, Greenwood." Blake winked. "Just wait and see."

That night, Beth was rocked to sleep by the rhythm of the train. It rolled and rumbled all night, preventing her from ever really reaching the deep restful sleep she needed. Then in the early hours of the morning she sensed the movement stop and realised they must have reached Winnipeg.

Sitting up, she rolled up the blinds in front of the square window and was greeted by the uninspiring view of the platform at Union Station.

Sitting back on her pillows, she reached her arms up into a tension-releasing stretch and was texting her mum to say, *You'll never GUESS what I'm doing today...?* when there was a knock on her door.

Reaching over – because she didn't need to leave the bed to touch the door handle – she unlocked it and mumbled, "Come in."

A hand appeared, holding a mug of coffee. And then Blake's smiling face.

His hair was messy, sticking up in amusing tufts that she hadn't seen before, and he was more stubbled than usual. But the dimples were still there.

"Ready for the big day?" he asked, stepping inside and lingering in the small space between the wall and the bed.

Beth gestured for him to sit down and tucked her knees up under her chin. "I can't believe they're actually doing it."

"Me neither. But isn't it kind of wonderful?"

Beth traced her index finger around the rim of her coffee cup. "It is. Really wonderful."

Blake gestured to Beth's watch. "We better get a move on. Doors open at eight a.m. and the ceremony's at nine."

"Right. And how far is the church from here?"

"Not far. Mike's minister buddy is sending two cars to pick us up at eight thirty. So that Mike and Dot can travel separately."

"Dot? Do you have to give *everyone* a nickname?"

"Only people I like."

Beth gulped down her coffee and swung her legs out of bed, trying not to blush. "Okay. Well, I better go find *Dot* and help her get ready then, hadn't I?"

"You sure had. See you at the church?"

"See you at the church."

Three hours later, their small silver taxicab pulled up outside a small stone-built church with a triangular roof.

Beside her, Doris wasn't even looking a tiny bit nervous. Her hair was loose, hanging in beautiful silvery curtains around her face, and her outfit was simple – a plain beige skirt with a cobalt blue blouse, a pearl necklace, and low-heeled pumps.

Beth had chosen a black dress with blue shoes that matched Doris's blouse and, as always, her birthstone pendant.

In the doorway of the church, Blake was waiting for

them. When Beth saw him, her heart did a little skip and a jump, and she instantly felt herself begin to blush.

"My, my," whispered Doris. "He scrubs up well, doesn't he?"

Beth couldn't reply; her mouth was dry and her tongue felt too heavy.

Blake waved and stepped forward to take Doris's arm. "Morning ladies. Dot, you look absolutely beautiful." He glanced over Doris's head at Beth and smiled sincerely at her, capturing her eyes with his and not letting them go. "So do you, Beth."

What Beth should have replied was, *My goodness. You are stunningly handsome*, because Blake was wearing dark grey trousers, a white shirt, and a thin black tie. He looked so good it was almost as if he'd just stepped straight off a movie set. But she didn't. Instead she said, "The shirt got an upgrade, I see."

Blake smiled at her cheekily. "Purely for your benefit, Greenwood."

At the door to the church, they stopped and Doris patted Blake's arm. "Now, please don't feel you have to agree to this. But I was wondering whether you might accompany me down the aisle? I'm a little worried my legs will give way with all the excitement."

Blake's lips spread into a pearly-white grin. "I would be honoured, Dot."

And so, Beth went inside and waited in the pews at the front, just behind Mike, until the doors opened and Doris entered. Slowly, with Blake steadying her, she walked towards Mike. All the while, smiling as if she was looking at the love of her life.

At the altar, Blake kissed her on the cheek and passed her hand to Mike. Then he stood beside Beth.

As Mike and Doris said, "I do," Blake reached out for Beth's hand, and she let him hold it. Because what they were witnessing was beautiful, and he was the only person in the world she could imagine experiencing it with.

CHAPTER SIXTEEN

From the church, they were whisked back to the about-to-depart train, where they sat in the dining car together and ordered champagne.

All four of them were almost giddy with excitement, and after lunch Beth persuaded Doris and Mike to let her take some wedding pictures of them out on the viewing platform and in the lounge car. In the centre of the car, Blake announced to the other passengers that these two sprightly young souls were newlyweds, and asked all the ladies present to gather and catch the bouquet.

Reluctantly, Beth handed him her camera and slipped into position. With her back to them, Doris said, "Ready, ladies? One... two... three..." then tossed her small lace-tied bunch of roses over her shoulder. A woman to Beth's right caught it and looked gleefully at her partner, who smiled and tutted, "Don't go getting any ideas."

As Beth took her camera back, Blake rolled his eyes at her and said loudly, "Dot, I told you to aim for Beth. What are you playing at?"

Somehow, amidst the laughter and the celebrations, the day quickly disappeared. And before they knew it, they were sitting in the lounge after dinner and Doris was yawning. Beside her, Mike was asleep with his head resting on her shoulder.

"Mike," she nudged. "Michael. Time we retired and left the youngsters to it, I think."

"Indeed," muttered Mike, gingerly getting to his feet. "Goodnight you two. And thank you."

At the door, Doris paused and turned back. "Have a good evening my dears... and don't do anything we wouldn't do."

Beth and Blake glanced at one another. "That doesn't leave us with many options, Dot," Blake replied, winking at her.

"Precisely," she said, winking back.

Slowly, as the sky outside darkened, the lounge car began to empty until it was just Blake and Beth.

Beth sat back and smoothed down her dress. "I really should go change. This isn't particularly train-friendly."

"It looks gorgeous, though."

"Is this you being friendly?" Beth asked, tilting her head to one side.

"Of course," he replied.

"And holding my hand in the ceremony...?"

"It was an emotional moment." Blake was rubbing the back of his neck sheepishly, but still smiling.

Beth looked up at the clock. "I might head to my cabin and edit these photos."

"Good idea. It's been a long day."

"A great day." Beth smiled, standing up and putting her camera strap over her shoulder.

"Can I escort you back, Ma'am?" Blake extended his arm and wiggled it at her.

"I suppose so." She looped her arm through his.

At their cabin doors, they paused and Blake let go of her. "Goodnight, Greenwood." The corridor was dark, except for the moonlight that was streaming in through the windows beside them.

"Goodnight, Blake." She was trying not to think about how good he looked in his crisp white shirt. They were standing close, so close she could smell his cologne and feel the warmth of his hand as it lingered close to hers.

They were swaying gently from side to side, jostled by the motion of the train, and as it lurched over a join in the tracks, Beth felt herself almost lose her balance. Blake steadied her. He was holding her by the elbows. Her hands were by his waist. She wanted to slide her arms around his back and pull him closer. But then, a few doors down, someone's cabin door opened and light flooded out into the hallway.

Beth stepped back and unlocked her door. "See you tomorrow, O'Brien. I'll look forward to being reunited with the checked shirt."

Day Ten - The Canadian

The day after the wedding, Beth stayed in her cabin until mid-morning writing her next article. Of course, it was about Doris and Mike so before submitting it she wanted to make sure they didn't mind. She wasn't sure either of them had told their children or grandchildren and didn't want to make the news public until they had.

For a while, after she woke, she'd expected Blake to arrive with a coffee. But he hadn't. Perhaps he was doing the same as her – enjoying watching the scenery go by and trying to write.

Beside her, her phone vibrated. It was her mum; she'd emailed over some pictures last night and was dying to hear what she thought of Doris and Mike's whirlwind romance.

What a superb story, Beth. How romantic. And wonderful to know that love can still blossom later in life. There's hope for me yet!

Beth paused with her thumbs above her phone's keyboard. Was her mum hinting that she wanted to find someone? Beth had never really thought about her mum being with anyone else and the idea niggled at her.

Putting the phone down, she slipped her shoes on and ventured out into the corridor.

She tapped on Blake's door, but he wasn't there. Eventually, she tracked him down in the sky carriage. Similar to the one on the *Rocky Mountaineer*, it was on the upper level of the train, with glass walls and a glass ceiling that allowed you to take in the spectacular views as the train trundled on through the Canadian wilderness.

Blake was sitting at the back with earphones in, staring absentmindedly out of the window.

Beth sat down beside him and nudged him.

"Morning," he said, turning off his music. "Nice lie-in?"

"I was writing," she replied. Then, because for some reason she just needed to talk about it and Blake was the only person she wanted to talk with, she said quickly, "I think my mum wants to start dating."

Blake frowned at her. "Okaaay?"

Beth showed him the text message. "See?"

Blake squinted at the phone screen. "Beth, I'm not sure this means she's ready to get back out there. But if she did, what's wrong with that?"

Beth felt herself bristle and sat up straighter in her seat. "I don't know. I suppose I just..."

"Thought she'd be alone forever?"

"She loved my dad."

"And I'm sure she still does. But she's human, Greenwood. We crave companionship. She might not find the same kind of love she had with your dad, but you don't want her to be alone forever do you?"

Beth folded her arms in front of her chest. She knew she was pouting; she'd wanted Blake to say, *Wow that's a little soon,* or, *I'm sure she's just joking around, she'll never be with anyone else.* But, despite feeling annoyed at him, she knew he was right. "No. Of course I don't want her to be alone."

Blake furrowed his brow and then started to smile. "Hang on... did you mean to say, 'You're absolutely right, Blake. How wise and emotionally astute you are...'?"

"No." Beth was trying to stop herself from smiling. She looked at him out of the corner of her eye. "I most certainly didn't."

"Hmm. Funny. Because it sounded like–"

"Okay. You're right. I was being childish and self-centred."

Blake softened a little and leaned closer. "It's not childish to feel weird about it. Don't beat yourself up for having feelings. But don't let them hold your mom back from being happy. Okay?"

"When did you get so wise?"

"I've always been wise. It just took you a while to get past my good looks and see me as something other than a piece of eye-candy." Blake wrinkled his nose at her and flexed his muscles.

Beth stood up and rolled her eyes at him. "Right. Well,

thanks for the chat. I need to find Doris and Mike. You coming?"

"Nah. I'll stay and enjoy the scenery. See you in a bit."

Downstairs, Beth found Doris and Mike in the lounge car and showed them her article. They were thrilled with it and adored the pictures, but all the while they were chatting to her and asking her questions about the competition, she couldn't take her mind off Blake. This whole trip, he'd been keen to follow her wherever she was going and do whatever she was doing. Almost every morning, he'd appeared out of nowhere with coffee and chatter. But this morning, he'd decided to do his own thing. And she wasn't sure she liked it.

Was it because she'd pulled away from him last night? Or did he just want a little alone time?

All day, she kept asking herself the same questions. A couple of times, she went back up to the sky carriage. The first time, Blake was dozing and didn't wake up and later he wasn't there.

By the time dinner rolled around, she'd spent so much time mulling it over that she'd lost her appetite. So, she went back to her cabin, finished her article, and went to sleep.

She'd been asleep a few hours when the jolting of the train woke her. It was just past midnight, but she couldn't get back to sleep.

She couldn't get Blake out of her head because, as much as she was trying not to admit it to herself, she'd missed him.

After ten days of being in one another's company almost twelve hours a day, she had felt lost without him. She'd tried to enjoy sitting by herself, spending time on her article, watching the rivers and mountains go by.

But the whole time she'd felt like something was missing.

And if she felt like this now, how on earth would she feel when their trip ended?

Maybe it was a good idea to try and put some distance between them.

Maybe it was sensible.

After all, friends didn't feel the need to be by one another's side *all* the time, did they? Friends didn't feel lost and twitchy and a little hollow without one another.

Tomorrow, she resolved, she would be better at it. She'd do her own thing, and let Blake do his. And by the time they reached Toronto, she'd be totally prepared for saying goodbye to him.

CHAPTER SEVENTEEN

Day Eleven –Approaching Toronto

*B*eth's last day aboard the train began with a gloomy view. Until now, they'd had nothing but spectacular weather – cold at night and in the mornings but sunny and almost cloud-free during the day. Today, however, as if the sky was reading her mood, it was sullen and misty.

Eventually, she persuaded herself to go for breakfast and found the newlywed Doris and Mike enjoying toast and porridge in the dining car. They gestured for Beth to join them so she did, purposefully not looking around to see if she could spot Blake.

"Are you quite alright, dear? You seem a little distracted." Doris was pouring tea from a small white teapot and looking at her intently with her watery blue eyes.

Beth tucked her hair behind her ear and put down her

toast. "Just thinking about what my next article should be about. We've got to submit another tomorrow night but there's nothing on the itinerary when we reach Toronto. Not until our last day and Niagara Falls. So it needs to be about the train really..." Trying to make herself sound more light-hearted than she felt, she continued, "And, after featuring you two love-birds, I'm just not sure what should follow it."

"Well," Mike said slowly – he always spoke as if he was choosing his words very, very carefully. "Why don't you talk to some other passengers? The wonderful thing about travel, to me, is the folks you meet on the way." Pausing, he looked at his wife and patted her hand. "And when you get talking, you realise that people have all sorts of marvellous stories to tell."

Beth bit her lower lip, contemplating what Mike had said. Then she felt herself start to smile; she could already see the article taking shape in her mind. "That, Mike, is an absolutely *brilliant* idea."

Proudly, Doris stroked Mike's forearm and said, "He doesn't say much. But what he does say is usually worth the wait."

"Thank you. Both of you." Beth stood up and gave Doris a kiss on the cheek. "I'll see you later."

"And if we see young Mr O'Brien... should we tell him you were looking for him?" Doris looked up and there was a glint in her eyes that said she knew exactly what Beth had been distracted about.

"No, no need. Thanks." Beth smiled, and before she

could sit back down and say, *Help me, Doris, I don't know what to do, I can't stop thinking about him...* she strode towards the other end of the dining car and through to the adjoining part of the train.

She spent the rest of the day, as Mike had suggested, making her way from one end of the train to the other, talking to the other passengers, taking their photographs, and making notes.

She met two very Canadian brothers in their fifties who'd never before ventured further than their hometown in Alberta but who had always promised one another that they'd see Canada by train before they turned sixty.

She met a young couple on their honeymoon, a family from England, some American backpackers, a French author, a tour group from Germany... and every single person she spoke to had a different reason for travelling, a different reason for wanting to see Canada by train, a different perspective on what the experience meant to them.

Later, back in her cabin, she uploaded the photographs to her iPad and converted them to black and white. As she scrolled through them, an excited flutter in her stomach told her that this would be her best article yet.

Thinking about it, she found herself glancing towards the wall that separated her cabin from Blake's. She wanted to tell him about it. She wanted to show him her pictures and tell him her ideas. She wanted to see his face, hear him call her 'Greenwood', and watch those ridiculous dimples of his when his lips spread into a cheeky grin.

All day, she'd expected to bump into him. She'd even kept her phone close by in case he texted her to ask where she was and if she wanted to have lunch or dinner together. But she'd heard nothing. And seen nothing. For almost twenty-four hours, she'd been utterly Blake-less. And she hated it.

Sighing and tidying away her things, she decided she needed to shower. At least that way she might be able to *wash* Blake out of her thoughts. Their en-suites were far too small to contain showers, but there was one at the end of the corridor. So, she grabbed her wash bag and her towel and padded barefoot towards it.

After three whole days on the train, she'd almost become accustomed to the swaying and rocking. But mid-shower, an extra-large bump on the tracks made the tiny shower cabin rock wildly from side to side. As she looked up, brushing water from her eyes, she realised that the clothes she'd hung on the back of the door had fallen off and – because the entire room was a wet-room with no shower tray, just a central drain in the middle of the floor – they were now soaked through with soapy shower water.

Reaching for the towel which, thankfully, she'd draped over the wash basin, Beth picked up her sodden clothes. "Oh flip," she muttered, tutting at herself.

Wrapping the towel around her still-damp body, she gingerly unfastened the door. Her cabin was mid-way down the corridor. It was ten p.m. The lights had been dimmed. She was pretty sure she could make it without anyone seeing her.

So, she bundled her wet clothes under her arm and made a run for it. She was looking behind her, checking that she hadn't dropped anything on the way – like underwear or socks – when she felt herself career into something solid. Instinctively, she put her hands out... and realised it was a person. A clothes-less person.

"Oh gosh, I'm so sorry..." She looked up, straight into the chest of Blake O'Brien. Naked from the waist up, he had a navy-blue towel slung around his middle and was blushing furiously.

"Beth?" Blake stepped back, put his hand on his hip, then down by his side, then sort of just held it across his middle.

"I was going to shower..."

"I was just coming back from the shower..."

They spoke at the same time, then laughed nervously.

Beth's hair was hanging loose and wet on her shoulders. She could feel droplets of water trickling down her neck. "I..."

"I haven't seen you all day," Blake said softly. "Have you been avoiding me?"

Beth looked up. She was trying to focus on his face, not his broad chest and the perfect line of hair that led down to his belly button. "A bit..." she replied. "But you started it. Yesterday."

Blake nodded. He still seemed unsure what to do with his hands. "I guess I did."

"Did I do something?" Her voice came out sounding small and slightly hurt.

"No, of course not. I just..." Blake rubbed the back of his neck and bit his lower lip. "When I'm around you, I find the whole 'friends' thing a little tricky."

"You do?" Beth was sure that her heart was going to leap right out of her chest. Surely, it was beating so loud he could hear it?

Blake looked down at his bare chest, then stepped back towards his cabin. "Maybe we should talk about this when we're fully clothed? Ten minutes? Up in the sky carriage?"

"I thought it was out of bounds at night."

Blake shrugged at her. "If we get caught, we'll just tell them we're famous journalists writing a very important article."

"Okay." She smiled, relief and excitement and trepidation rushing over her all at the same time. "See you up there."

When she reached the top of the stairs, she thought the sky carriage was empty. But then she spotted Blake at the back, dressed in his blue checked shirt, motioning for her to join him.

"There's no one else here," she whispered, sitting down next to him.

"Pretty nice, huh?" Blake replied.

Beth looked at him quickly, then looked up. "Wow. Look at the stars. I don't think I've ever seen them so bright."

"Beautiful," Blake whispered, but when Beth turned her head he wasn't looking up, he was looking at her.

"Blake," she said, angling her body so it was facing him. "What's happening here? We hated each other, then we nearly kissed, then we were friends, and now..."

Blake thought for a moment then slowly said, "I don't know. All I know is that when I'm around you, I want to be close to you. And when I'm not around you, I can't think about anything else." He took her hand in his, turning it over so he could stroke her palm. "And I never hated you, by the way."

"You didn't?"

"*Never.*"

"But you were so..."

"I was a jerk. Several times over. Do you want to know why?"

"Why?"

Blake laughed wryly at himself and shook his head. "Because you're stunning, and talented, and funny. And I was trying, in my misguided way, to impress you."

"Well," said Beth, tweaking his chin with her index finger and making him look at her. "It worked."

"Beth..."

"Blake. I know this can't go anywhere. I know we have to say goodbye in a few days. But, for now, could we maybe be a little more than friends?" She lowered her voice to a whisper. "Just for now?"

Blake brushed his fingers through her hair and let them

rest at the back of her neck. "I think I can do that," he whispered. Then, finally, he kissed her. He pressed his lips to hers and the world melted away.

It was just the two of them, under the stars, travelling across the moonlit plains. And she never wanted the kissing to end.

CHAPTER EIGHTEEN

Day Twelve – Toronto

Their train arrived in Toronto just after breakfast. Beth had woken early with butterflies in her stomach. Remembering the night before, she had placed her hand on the wall that divided her room from Blake's and whispered, "Just enjoy it, Beth. Don't think about the end of the competition. Just enjoy your time together."

On the platform, they said goodbye to Mike and Doris, promised to stay in touch, and watched as the couple hailed a cab and rode off together as husband and wife.

In the pick-up zone, Emily was waiting for them with coffee and hugs and an excited smile. "How *are* you both?! Beth, I can't even tell you how much we loved your piece on Mike and Doris. Blake, I'm surprised you let her have that one!"

Blake shrugged and glanced at Beth. She'd never thought of it that way before. She'd just written her piece and submitted it; she hadn't stopped to wonder why Blake hadn't written about it too. "Ah," he said, "that touchy feely stuff isn't my style."

"Well," Emily said, "there's still time. We need one article from you tonight and then another tomorrow. The big finale!"

"Niagara Falls is tomorrow?"

"Sure is. Now let's get you guys to your hotel so you can get used to being on non-moving ground, shall we? Blake, I know your apartment's only a few blocks away but Nomad are still happy to put you up in the fancy hotel, so I think you should take it."

"Absolutely. Never turn down a freebie, that's my motto."

"Great. Follow me, guys."

Beth was putting the finishing touches to her article about the train passengers when her phone buzzed.

Ms Greenwood, would you do me the honour of joining me for dinner this evening?

Holding her phone to her chest, she grinned, jigged her feet up and down, then replied.

I would love to, Mr O'Brien.

Meet you in the lobby at seven thirty?

Ball-gown or no ball-gown?

More than a towel, less than a ball-gown. No checked shirts.

Okay. See you there.

"This feels like a date," Beth whispered as they walked into the luxurious hotel dining room arm-in-arm.

"I think it is a date." Blake was wearing the same white shirt and grey trousers that he'd chosen for the wedding but, somehow, tonight he looked even better.

Beth too, had stuck with her wedding-guest outfit. Black dress, blue heels, and her pendant. Only, this time, she'd added a touch more makeup and a few extra sprays of perfume.

As they sat together, drinking wine and chatting and letting their fingers touch across the table, she felt – for the first time in such a long time – happy. Not just content or *okay*. Happy.

"My dad would have really liked you, Blake," she said, touching the pendant around her neck and looking up at him.

"He would?" Blake looked slightly taken aback.

"He'd have been impressed by your blog – what you've achieved with it – definitely."

Blake shook his head. "My blog is just *content* – your dad was a real writer. And that's what you should be too."

"Why'd you say that?"

"I've read your pieces, Beth. You were good before we

started the competition but something's happened since you got here. It's like you found out who you're supposed to be. And you're a *great* writer." He paused and smiled at her with a tilt of the head that said he was about to make a joke. "I mean, I do take some of the credit. It was my *critique* that helped you figure out the kind of stuff you really want to be writing..."

Beth nudged his leg playfully with her foot. "Well, I'll make sure to thank you when I win."

"Please do," he replied.

"You wouldn't mind if I beat you?"

"Actually..." He smiled and took her hand. "I'm praying that you do."

"No, you're not.'

"Seriously. I am. You deserve it *way* more than I do."

"You're just saying that because you're trying to stay in my good books."

"Maybe," he replied. "Maybe not."

"Well, it's not long before we find out. Last day tomorrow..." She took a sip from her wine glass and sat back in her chair, still fiddling with her necklace.

"You've worn that the whole trip. Is it special?" Blake gestured to it, being careful not to let his eyes linger too long.

"My dad gave it to me before my first ever trip abroad. I was twelve. It was a school trip to France, and I was *so* nervous. He said it would bring me good luck and remind me that he was always watching over me. It's my birth stone. I haven't taken it off since he died."

"He sounds like a wonderful man."

"He was." Beth smiled, remembering her father's twinkling eyes. "You know, he loved Niagara Falls. He went once. A long, long time ago. Have you been?"

"As a kid."

"My dad wanted his ashes to be scattered there. Of course, it was impossible. But he said Niagara was his favourite place in Canada." Beth tapped her fingernails on the side of her glass and looked out at the city. She'd been looking forward to seeing Niagara Falls ever since she'd heard it was where the trip would finish. But now that the end was so close, all she could think about was that in a couple of days she'd be on her way back to England.

She'd say goodbye to Blake. Get on a plane. Fly over the ocean. And then she'd be back in Oxford. Rainy, sleepy, quiet Oxford. Harry would be there, waiting to pick over the ruins of their relationship. Jo would be there, desperate to know everything about the trip. And her mum would be there, hugging her and welcoming her back. And then, a few weeks later, she'd receive an email from Emily or some top-bod at Nomad, telling her that Blake had won the competition. And she'd have to watch him blog his way around the world. Without her. He'd probably meet someone. A kindred spirit who would accompany him to all the exotic places he'd ever dreamed of.

"Beth?" Blake waved a hand in front of her face. "Hello? Earth to Beth?"

"Sorry," she shook her head and tried to re-orientate herself. "I was just thinking about what happens next."

"Next?"

She caught his eyes, then looked quickly away and cleared her throat. "With us."

Blake breathed in slowly and squeezed her hand. "What do you want to happen?" He was looking at her as if he might be able to find the answer written on her face.

She wanted to say, *I want us to be together.* But she couldn't. She understood that Blake liked her. But how much? They'd shared one almost-kiss and one actual kiss - it was hardly the stuff great love stories were made of. And yet, she felt as if they were both dreading saying goodbye.

The Blake O'Brien sitting in front of her now was so different from the one she'd met at the beginning of the trip, but she still couldn't work out what he was really thinking. So, tentatively, looking down at their entwined fingers instead of into his eyes, she said, "I'll miss you." Because that was all she knew for certain.

"I'll miss you too."

Beth took her hand back slowly and tried to smile. "No you won't, you'll be travelling around the world with your buddy Karl. You'll be far too happy to miss me."

"Well..." Blake paused and took a large sip of red wine from his glass. "I wouldn't *have* to take Karl."

Beth didn't speak. She just waited. Waited for him to say it...

"Beth. I was thinking..."

"Yes?"

Blake drummed his fingers on the table. Then sat up. "I was thinking that we should head to bed soon. Need to be fresh for our last day. Don't we?"

Beth felt her throat constrict. A lump that was threatening to turn to tears was creeping up into her mouth. She really thought he was going to say it... *Let's travel together, no matter who wins.* But clearly she was wrong.

"Yes. We do." She stood up and grabbed her handbag, leaving her unfinished wine on the table. "Goodnight Blake."

"Beth..."

She turned back. Her hands were trembling.

"Goodnight." Blake smiled thinly at her, then looked away, down at his drink.

Beth didn't reply. And as soon as she reached the elevator, she let herself cry.

Emily had arranged a cab to take them to Niagara, and when Beth ventured into the lobby the next morning Blake was already there waiting.

He smiled at her bashfully and lingered in front of her, as if he wasn't sure whether to be affectionate or not. Were they supposed to be acting like two people who'd been on a date last night? Or were they back to being friends?

Beth didn't know either, so she just patted him awkwardly on the arm and said, "Morning."

Emily, clearly not noticing anything odd between them, ushered them towards the cab. "When you're ready, just call me and I'll send someone to pick you up. Have a *great* last day."

"Excited?" Blake asked as the driver pulled out of the hotel's front courtyard and into a heavy stream of early-morning traffic.

"Nervous." Beth reached for her pendant and rubbed it slowly between her fingers.

"No need to be nervous, Greenwood. You won't care about the height when you see them."

Beth smiled wryly at him and tried to fight the urge to sigh. "It's not that. It's just... finally seeing something I've dreamed about for so long... I'm worried I've built it up too much... that I'll be disappointed."

"Trust me, Beth, you won't be disappointed."

CHAPTER NINETEEN

*T*heir cab dropped them in the parking lot and, as they walked towards the Welcome Centre, the sound of fast-moving water filled Beth's ears. It was a bright day. The sky was almost cloud-less, and as she caught a glimpse of the water her skin began to tingle with anticipation.

Finally, she saw them. The enormous, thundering waterfalls that her father had talked about. She and Blake were standing level with the top of the falls. It was early and, so far, there were only a few tourists leaning over the black railings and peering down below.

Beth couldn't contain her excitement; she broke away from Blake and jogged towards them, so overwhelmed that she could barely even bring herself to reach for her camera. Huge cascades of foaming water tumbled down into the pool below.

They were bigger than she'd imagined and Blake was right. She wasn't disappointed. They were powerful. So powerful they almost took her breath away.

Finally, she took some photographs, but they didn't seem to capture what she was seeing.

Below, the Maiden of the Mist tourist boat was making its first trip of the day out to view the Falls from below, and it was only when Blake pointed at it and said, "You want to go get booked onto the next boat?" that she realised he'd caught her up and was standing beside her.

"Absolutely," she replied.

In the queue for the boat, they were handed fashionable blue plastic ponchos and Blake immediately took a selfie of them with their hoods up and their sunglasses on, looking utterly ridiculous.

On deck, they were warned that as they got close to the Falls it would get *very* loud and *very* wet. But where some passengers moved towards the middle of the boat to stay dry, Beth hurried to the side, desperate to feel the spray on her face.

The Maiden of the Mist headed straight for the centre of the Falls, then turned so that they were sailing parallel with them on the way back.

The entire time, Beth stood with her arms outstretched, not caring that her blue poncho was letting water in, not caring that her makeup was running and her hair dripping wet, not caring that her shoes were sodden, just letting the water touch her skin and smiling from ear-to-ear.

"You're crazy," Blake tutted at her, chuckling as he stood back from the side. "You're drenched!"

"I know!" She laughed. Then, waving her camera at him, shouted above the sound of the water, "Good job this is waterproof!"

They were almost at the end of their voyage when Beth decided to try and take a picture of the helm of the boat with the Falls in the background. Leaning over the side, she angled her camera so that the boat took up half of the frame, took a few shots with the boat in focus and a few with the Falls in focus, then - as a steward tutted at her and asked her to keep her arms inside the boat - tucked herself back inside. As she did, she felt something tug at her neck. She reached up for her pendant but, before she realised what was happening, she felt a *snap*; it had got caught on the railing as she leaned over it. She grabbed for it, but her fingers were still damp and the chain slipped right through her hands.

"No!" She cried out and lurched forward, almost hauling herself over the side after it.

Blake grabbed her arm. "What is it? What happened?"

Turning to him, she could barely get the words out. Instead, she reached for the empty spot on her chest and looked towards the edge of the boat. "It broke..." The words came out small and quivering.

"Oh Beth, I'm so sorry."

"It's gone."

"Hey," Blake pulled her into his arms and kissed her forehead. For a moment, he didn't say anything. Just held her tight. Then he whispered, "Hey, it's okay. Listen..." He cupped her face in his hands and stroked the tears that were falling down her cheeks.

Beth looked away. The pain in her heart was almost physical.

Blake dipped his head to catch her eyes. "Your dad wanted his ashes to be scattered here, right?"

Beth nodded slowly. "Yes. He did."

He stroked the spot just below her throat, where her pendant usually sat nestled against her skin. "Well, now a little piece of him is here."

Beth let Blake's words settle inside her. It was the perfect thing to say. The only thing that could have made her feel better. "Thank you," she whispered, wrapping her arms around his waist and letting herself lean into him. "Thank you, Blake."

After slipping off their ponchos and sitting in the sun to dry off, they got take-out sandwiches and coffee and walked along the top of the Falls.

Beth's ribcage felt tight and tingly. After the high of seeing the waterfalls and riding beneath the spray, the heartbreak of losing her pendant had left her feeling anxious and out of place.

Blake's words had helped. She liked the thought of her father getting his wish - a little bit of him being carried away with the rush of the Falls. But at the same time, she felt like she'd lost a piece of him. And now that their final excursion was over, she couldn't shake the feeling that she was losing Blake too.

Both of them were unusually quiet as they walked. Any other day, they'd either be exchanging barbs or talking about other things they wanted to see and do when they travelled the world. But now, there was something sombre in the air between them.

"Beth..." Blake stopped and leaned against the railings with his back to the river. "It seems a shame to just head back to the hotel and squirrel ourselves away to write."

Beth tilted her head at him. "What else do you have in mind?"

"Well, my hometown's not far. I think you'd like it. It's pretty quaint."

"Niagara on the Lake?" She remembered him mentioning it when Emily had first interviewed them.

Blake nodded. He was wringing his hands together nervously, as if he had something else to say but couldn't quite manage it.

"What is it?" Beth raised her sunglasses so she could narrow her eyes at him.

Blake ran a finger around the collar of his shirt. His neck was flushed. "It's, ah, well... I was talking to my mom last night and she said that, if we had time, she'd love to meet you." He spoke quickly, throwing his words together as if it would make them less impactful somehow.

Beth couldn't help smiling. "You spoke to your mum about me?"

Shrugging, Blake's mouth twitched into a bashful smile. "A bit."

"Sure. Let's do it. I'd love to meet Mr and Mrs O'Brien."

Niagara on the Lake was the quintessential adorable Canadian town. Tree-lined streets, red brick buildings, a clock tower at one end of the main street and even horse-drawn carriages taking loved-up couples on rides.

"Fancy it?" Blake nodded towards a big shiny carriage and a beautiful grey horse. The driver was wearing a top hat, a white shirt, and a waistcoat. Blake put one foot on the side of the carriage and hopped up to whisper something in his ear. The driver smiled, nodded, and then said to Beth, "Welcome aboard Ma'am."

Blake reached out his hand and helped her up. The seats were red and soft, and as she sat down Blake unashamedly put his arm around her.

"Is this another date?" she asked.

"Yeah," he replied. "I think it is."

Our second and our last, Beth thought. But she didn't say it out loud. Instead, she leaned into Blake's shoulder and decided that if this was their last afternoon together she needed to do nothing more than just enjoy every second of it – and ignore the gloomy tugging sensation in the pit of her stomach that kept reminding her she'd soon be hundreds of miles away from him.

The scenery of Blake's beautiful hometown certainly did a good job of distracting her from that feeling. The sun was warm. Everywhere they looked, flowers were in bloom. And Beth felt as if she was riding through a movie set — too idyllic to be a place that people actually lived in.

They'd almost finished their ride around town, when the driver - instead of heading back to the main thoroughfare - headed off down a side street. Then, a few minutes later, he stopped outside a large red-brick town house with flower-covered railings on its porch.

"Your stop, Sir." He tipped his hat at Blake.

Blake reached into his wallet, handed over the last of his spending money from Nomad, and then helped Beth down onto the pavement. Waving at the house in front of them, he said, "This is it. Home."

Beth smiled. "Blake O'Brien, you really are something out of a fairy-tale."

Blake slipped his hand into hers, and she thought he might be about to lean over and kiss her, when the door to the town house opened and a short sharp squeal filled the air.

"Blake!"

They looked up to see a short, blonde-haired woman in smart trousers and a white blouse waving at them. She hurried down the steps, flung open the front gate, and pulled Blake into an embrace. Then let him go and did the same to Beth.

She clutched Beth's hands between hers. "Beth Greenwood, it is a *pleasure* to finally meet you. I've been devouring your articles. They're just fantastic."

Coughing and raising his eyebrows, Blake said, "Gee, thanks Mom."

But his mum shook her head and playfully pinched his cheek. "Oh, and yours of course my darling." Turning back to Beth and putting her arm around her, she pulled her close and led her through the front gate and up the steps to the house. "Come inside and meet my husband Mark. He's dying to meet you. Blake's told us *so* much about you. We've never heard him so enthusiastic about a girl before."

Beth looked back and saw Blake visibly cringing. "Mom," he said, sounding almost like an embarrassed teenager.

But his mother simply waved her hand at him and tutted, "Oh Blake. Don't be silly. Beth must know that you like her. You don't take just any old person on a horse-drawn carriage ride, do you?" Looking at Beth, she leaned in and whispered, "He likes to pretend he's macho, but he's a big softy really."

"Really?" Beth glanced back at Blake and grinned at him. "I never would have guessed."

CHAPTER TWENTY

*A*fter dinner, during which Blake's parents took great delight in regaling Beth with almost every embarrassing tale from his high-school years, they disappeared to the kitchen to do the dishes and left the two of them to write their final articles.

Spreading out at the dining room table, Blake drummed his fingers on his keyboard and said, "Wow. So the pressure's really on now, huh?"

Beth swallowed purposefully and tried to smile. She suddenly felt overwhelmingly close to tears. This was it. The last evening she'd spend in Blake's company.

For close to an hour, they sat opposite one another, typing and re-typing, sighing, and making minimal progress.

Beth was finding it almost impossible to concentrate; a voice in her head was whispering *Ask him. Just ask him. Ask him if he wants to see you again. Ask him if he wants to travel the world with you. If you don't ask, you'll never know...*

Eventually, she scraped her chair back from the table and said, "Is it okay if I go make some coffee? I'm struggling to focus."

"Good idea. I'll do it." Blake headed towards the door. "No peeking though." He gestured to his laptop.

"I promise," Beth replied. But as soon as Blake was out of the room, an overwhelming sense of curiosity took hold of her. Would Blake be sticking to his tried-and-tested *listicle* for their final submission? Or something else? Emily had told them to write about their 'overall' experience. So, would Blake have mentioned her? Because she had been struggling to sum up her experience without mentioning him.

Against her better judgement, Beth stood up and moved cautiously around the table until she was leaning over the back of Blake's empty chair, staring at his screen. The document he had open was a transcript of the notes he'd dictated at Niagara Falls. But there was another just behind it.

She clicked on it. And started reading.

When I first met Beth Greenwood, I had no idea she was the daughter of the infamous travel writer Charles Greenwood. Unassumingly beautiful, straight away she came across as someone who had something to prove. So, of course, when I discovered her heritage, all the pieces fell into place.

My friendship with Beth has shaped my experience in

this competition more than I thought possible. I came into this trip knowing who I am and what I want - from life and from my blog - but Beth didn't even know herself.

In the beginning, she veered between wanting to be independent and wanting to honour her father's memory. As the days went on, she seemed to find herself.

Beth told me that she doesn't want to write what's commercially viable. She wants to write from the heart. And that really stuck with me. So, I thought I'd try it. I thought, for once, I'd try writing something with feeling.

And I don't think I've ever felt more than I did when we were standing beneath Niagara Falls, on the Maiden of the Mist, wearing silly blue ponchos and covered in spray.

To me, it seemed as if Beth was finally saying goodbye to her father. Niagara Falls was a place he'd always told her stories about - one of the first places he visited when he started travelling - and somewhere they'd dreamed of seeing together... ... ...

Beth stopped reading and stumbled backwards, the force of her emotions hitting her like a punch in the guts. Blake's final article was about her. And not just her. It was about her and her father.

Not only had he taken what was unique to her - her style, her openness, her emotion - he'd used it to expose details she'd never shared with anyone else.

A wave of nausea swept from her head to her toes and, in a daze, she moved back to her side of the table. Sitting down, she reached for her bag and started to shove her things back into it.

Then, before Blake could return, she ran to the front door and out onto the street. And she kept running until she reached the centre of town.

Panting and shaking, she called Emily and asked if she could send a cab to fetch her.

As she waited, she was almost certain that Blake would - at any second - catch up with her. But she couldn't bear the thought of seeing him. She'd persuaded herself to trust him. She'd even been about to tell him she had feelings for him. And yet the whole time, he was no different from the arrogant, self-centred, egotistical jerk she'd met two weeks ago. The kind of person who'd do anything to win. Even if it meant exposing her inner-most thoughts and feelings to the world.

How could she ever have let herself fall for Blake O'Brien?

Back at her hotel, Beth turned off her phone and through tears she thought would never stop coming wrote her final piece. It was awful. She was sure of it. But she didn't care anymore. All she wanted was to go home.

That night, she barely slept. And at six a.m., instead of getting ready to meet Emily and Blake for their final goodbye breakfast, she left a message for Emily at reception, called a cab and went straight to the airport.

There, safely in the departure lounge, she switched on her phone. Twenty missed calls from Blake. And three voicemail messages.

Beth, where are you? What happened? Mom said she saw you leave? What's going on?

Beth, I'm getting worried now, please call me.

In the third message, his voice was different. Shaky. Upset.

Beth... please call me back. I'm not sure what happened... I... I think maybe you saw what was on my laptop? I need to explain. Please, Beth?

Without hesitating, Beth deleted them, turned her phone back off, and shoved it deep into her handbag.

CHAPTER TWENTY-ONE

TWELVE HOURS LATER

*B*eth's mum and Jo were, as promised, waiting for her at the airport. Beth flung herself into their arms, breathed them in, listened to them tell her they loved her and they'd missed her and that they were so, so proud of her. And all the way home in the car, she managed to hold herself together. She told them about the trains, and the bears, and Niagara Falls. But when they sat down at the kitchen table and Jo said, "Okay, so now tell us what we really want to know... what was the hunky Blake really like?" Beth burst into tears.

Assuming she was heart-broken over Harry, Beth's mum immediately put the kettle on and gave her an enormous hug. "There, there, sweet girl. It's okay," she whispered, stroking her daughter's hair. "It's for the best. You both want different things."

Beth sniffed and wiped her eyes, pulling away and - between sobs - muttering, "I know... It's... not Harry I'm upset about."

Jo and Beth's mum exchanged a perplexed glance.

"It's not?" Jo asked, sounding slightly impressed.

"It was awful, and I shouldn't have broken up with him on the phone like that. But as soon as I'd said it... you know, told him I didn't want to marry him, I felt better."

"Then what is it sweetheart?" Her mum sat down next to her and squeezed her hand.

Beth looked at both of them. She didn't want to say it out loud, because it sounded foolish and fanciful and like something a misguided teenager would say. "I think I fell in love with Blake O'Brien."

Jo's hand involuntarily flew to her mouth. Mum opened her mouth, closed it again, then said, "Well that explains the tears. After spending all that time together, you must be missing him already."

Beth shook her head, wiping her cheek with the back of her hand. "No. I mean, yes, I do." Her stomach tightened at the thought of how far away he was. "But the thing is... he betrayed me. Completely. When we met, I thought he was arrogant and mean and awful but the more I got to know him the more I liked him."

Jo's features had set into an angry and protective scowl. "Did he cheat on you, Beth?"

Beth's eyes widened. "No. Nothing like that."

"Then what happened, Beth?" Her mum patted her gently between the shoulder blades.

"On the last night, we were writing our final pieces and he went to make coffee. We were at his parents' house and..."

"His parents?" Her mother sounded oddly impressed.

"They live near Niagara Falls. They made us dinner. And when Blake went to fetch coffee, I looked at his laptop."

"Uh oh," breathed Jo.

"He was writing about me."

Mum and Jo exchanged another confused glance.

"All of his other articles were these short snappy touristy pieces. But, all of a sudden, he changed. He was writing like me. And *about* me." She looked at her mother and tears started to well up in the corners of her eyes again. "And about dad."

Mum wrapped her in a deep hug and kissed her forehead. "Oh Beth, I'm sorry."

"It was so personal. Things I've never told anyone. And he's just put them there, for the whole world to see."

Mum was shaking her head and patting Beth on the arm. But Jo was still frowning.

"Did you ask him about it?" She was reaching for her phone as she asked the question.

"No," Beth replied, stubbornly. "I just left. He tried to call me but I didn't answer."

Jo reached out, handing Beth her phone. "Beth, this is Blake's article. Nomad put your final entries online this morning. It doesn't say anything about you. It's just a list of reasons why seeing Canada by train is the best way to travel."

Beth grabbed the phone and started reading. Jo was right. This wasn't the article she'd seen on his computer.

"He must have changed his mind..." she breathed.

"Or he never intended to publish it," Jo said.

"Beth, my love. Why didn't you give him a chance to explain?" Mum was trying to be gentle with her, but clearly thought she'd been rash by simply running away and ignoring Blake's attempts to call her.

"I..." her words trailed off, because she didn't know why. Maybe because it was easier to believe he'd betrayed her than face up to the fact that she was dreading leaving him? Or because she'd trusted him with her deepest thoughts and the idea that he was going to share them with the rest of the world was just too painful? "What have I done?" she asked, looking from Jo to her mum. "What on earth have I done?"

***

For nearly three hours that evening, Jo and her mum consoled, cajoled, and cuddled Beth, bringing her cups of tea and trying to persuade her that perhaps she should pick up the phone and call Blake to straighten it all out. But Beth was adamant that there was no point.

"He hasn't emailed me, Mum. Or texted since I walked out. I left without saying goodbye. I just left. I didn't give him the chance to explain, I just ran away. So, even if he did have feelings for me before I'm pretty sure they're gone now."

"Beth," her mum was speaking softly and tentatively, "I'm just going to say one more thing and then we'll eat ice cream, watch a trashy film, and go to bed, okay?"

Beth nodded. "Okay."

"In all the time you were with Harry, I never saw you like this. You were fond of him, I know. But I don't think you ever really *loved* him. Not the crazy, head-over-heels, I can't breathe without you kind of love that I felt for your father."

Beth looked at Jo, who was nodding in agreement.

"And yet this handsome Canadian, who you've only known for two weeks, has made you cry like a heart-broken teenager."

"And that's a good thing?" Beth sniffed and wiped her puffy eyes with her sleeve.

"Yes. I think it is. Because if you're this upset at the thought of losing him, he must be worth keeping hold of."

"But I've known Blake for *two weeks* - it's crazy."

Her mum shrugged. "Love is crazy."

Beth looked at Jo, then her mum. "So, what do I do?"

CHAPTER TWENTY-TWO

TWO WEEKS LATER

For two weeks, Beth barely left the house.

The morning after she told her mum and Jo about what happened with Blake, she took their advice and emailed him. She wrote that she was sorry for leaving the way she did, and that she wanted so badly to talk to him, and she asked him to call her, or text, or email.

But just like the very first email she'd sent him, back before they even met, Blake ignored it.

Fourteen days went by, and she heard nothing from him. He wasn't updating his blog. He wasn't posting to social media. It was like he'd disappeared.

Fourteen days in Canada had gone by in the blink of an eye, and yet fourteen days back in Oxford felt like an eternity. And Beth couldn't understand why her feelings for Blake had grown so quickly and yet refused to fade.

Two weeks after leaving Toronto, she felt just as raw and devastated as she had then.

And now the day was approaching when she'd discover who had won the competition. Emily had emailed to say that any day now the judges should be making their decision, but Beth almost emailed her back saying not to bother; she knew Blake would be the winner. She'd known it from the start.

She was standing in front of her bedroom mirror, wondering whether she could get away with another day of not washing her hair, when she heard the doorbell ring downstairs. Peeking out of her bedroom window, she stepped quickly back behind the curtain when she saw who it was; it was Harry. Dressed in his customary work suit, despite the fact it was Monday and he didn't work Mondays, he stood stiffly on the doorstep as if he was waiting for an interview.

Without letting herself be seen, Beth opened the window a little and shouted, "I'll be right down." Then she hurriedly swapped her pyjamas for jeans and a white sweater, scraped her hair back into a ponytail, and went to let him in.

Sitting at the kitchen table, Harry somehow looked different. His face wasn't as familiar as it had been, and there was something strange in his expression that she hadn't seen before.

Beth handed him a coffee and sat down opposite him.

"Welcome home," he said, with a thin but sincere smile.

"Thanks."

"I followed your trip on the Nomad blog. I read your articles. They were great, Beth. Really great."

Beth shifted uncomfortably in her chair. "Thank you. I didn't expect you to read them."

Harry blinked at her. "Of course I read them." Then he sighed. "Beth, I'm so sorry."

For a moment, Beth's stomach tightened and she found herself praying that Harry wasn't about to try and get back together. But then he said, "I think for a while now we've both known things weren't right. But we shouldn't have talked about it on the phone."

Beth exhaled slowly and nodded. "I know. I'm so sorry. I didn't mean it to come out the way it did, or when it did."

Harry lifted his hand to stop her talking. "Please don't apologise."

She didn't. And then for a couple of too-long seconds neither of them spoke. "I still care about you, Harry." She said the words quietly, without looking at him. "We just want—"

"Different things," he finished.

Beth looked up and Harry smiled at her.

"It doesn't make us bad people, Beth. I want stability and you want excitement. I want to settle down in Oxford, you want to see the world. And for too long we've been trying to change one another. That's not what love is about. Love is..." he stopped, chewing his lip as he tried to think of how to finish his sentence.

"Love is about finding your missing piece. The one

person whose dreams fit with yours. Who makes you feel like anything is possible." Beth tried not to let her voice waver as she remembered the way Blake had looked when he said those words.

"Yes," said Harry. "I suppose it is."

Harry didn't stay at the house long. He drank his coffee, agreed that when the dust had settled they could try to be friends, and then left to go and scope out potential new premises for Cooper's new branch.

After he'd gone, Beth went to her father's writing shed. And this time, for the first time since she was a little girl, she sat in his green armchair.

Curling her feet up beneath her, she looked up at his post-cards and maps and cut-out newspaper clippings of book reviews. "Oh Dad," she whispered. "If you were here, you'd know how to fix this. I know you would."

Instinctively, she reached for her necklace and when her fingers met with nothing but the cool skin below her throat, she winced.

"I'm so sorry I lost it."

She sighed and leaned back into the softness of the chair.

"Dad, if I'm meant to be with Blake... give me a sign? Just a little sign?"

She sat for a moment, watching for a ray of sunlight, or a

butterfly, or a white feather that she could label a message from her father. But nothing came.

She might have started crying again, but the crunch of footsteps on the gravel driveway made her stand and stick her upper body out into the garden.

Bobbing above the garden fence, she could just make out the head of their postman.

"Paul?" She walked over to the fence and climbed up on a garden chair.

"Oh Beth, I was about to leave this with a neighbour. Just an envelope, but it's a special delivery so needs to be signed for."

Beth reached up and squiggled her name on Paul's electronic pad. Then he handed her a small brown envelope and continued on his round.

Turning it over in her hands, Beth took the envelope back into the shed and sat down on the edge of her dad's armchair.

She didn't recognise the handwriting. But the stamp said: TORONTO.

Her fingers trembled as she peeled back the sealed flap on the back of the envelope. She reached inside and drew out a bundle of what looked like postcards, tied together with an elastic band.

Slowly, she removed it. The first postcard was from Jasper, the picture on the front showing the infamous aerial tramway as it glided up into the mountains. On the other side, handwritten, was the message:

Dear Beth,

Maybe I won't ever give you this. Maybe it will stay hidden and secret for the rest of our days because it's just a little bit crazy. But maybe not. Maybe one day I'll be brave enough to tell you that today is the day I fell in love with you.

I'm not the world's greatest romantic. In fact, as you know, my main tactic when I like a girl is to be mean and sarcastic and make an idiot of myself.

But today something changed. And I want to remember it. Forever.

Yours,

Blake

Beth was gripping the postcard so tightly that her fingernails were leaving little moon-shaped impressions on its surface. But this wasn't the only one. There were more.

She leafed through them. One for every place they'd visited after they left Jasper.

THE *CANADIAN* TRAIN

Dear Beth,

I can't think of anything better than being on a train with you for four days. Maybe by the end of this trip I'll have changed your mind about me. Here's hoping.

So much more than your friend,

Blake

EDMONTON

Dear Beth,

You looked beautiful today. You are impulsive, disorganised, and insanely talented with your words and your camera. I think you're starting to like me. Maybe one day we'll do a Doris and Mike and plan a ridiculously impromptu wedding?

Blake

WINNIPEG

Dear Beth,

Of all the things I thought I'd do on this trip, walking an eighty-five year old down the aisle for her shotgun wedding was not one of them. But it was probably the most wonderful thing I've ever witnessed. Seeing Doris and Mike loving each other so much, and taking such a huge risk, made me feel like maybe there's hope for you and me? Maybe it's not crazy to love someone you've only known for a handful of days?

Blake

THE SKY DOME

Dear Beth,

If I was a romantic guy, I'd have planned the sky dome and the stars and our first proper kiss. But I'm hopeless at romance, so I winged it. And, hey, it seems it turned out pretty good.

Kissing you under the stars will stay with me forever, even if you never love me back and leave me alone and heartbroken and unfit for loving another woman as long as I live.

No pressure.

Blake

TORONTO

Dear Beth,

We are almost done. I haven't told you how I feel about you. I haven't asked you the question I'm dying to ask you. I'm a coward. Perhaps I'll just give you these postcards and let them do the talking for me. Or perhaps I'll chicken out and regret it forever.

Blake

NIAGARA-ON-THE-LAKE

Dear Beth,

You've been gone for over a week. And I'm sitting here in my parents' living room, still missing you, still head-over-heels in love with you.

I know you think I was going to use what I wrote about you for my article. I would never do that. If I'd been honest with you about my feelings, maybe you'd have trusted me. But maybe you wouldn't. I was kind of a jerk for sixty percent of our trip.

I hope the gesture enclosed in this envelope will show you that deep down I'm a good guy. The kind of guy who would go to the ends of the earth for you (it did take three trips on The Maiden of the Mist and an almost-illegal climb to an out-of-bounds, potentially fatal, cluster of rocks to find but, you know, no pressure to be impressed.)

Yours, if you'll have me,

Blake

With shaking hands, Beth set down the postcards and peered inside the envelope.

At the bottom, there was a small blue velvet pouch. She lifted it out and prised it open.

And there it was - her necklace. The one she thought

she'd never see again. Holding it in the palm of her hand, her heart began to swell. A small fragment was broken. A little piece was missing. A piece that was still at Niagara.

Slowly, a grin spread over Beth's face. She stood up, spread out her arms, looked up towards the heavens and shouted, "Thank you, Dad! Thank you!" Then she whispered, "That's one heck of a sign, old man. One heck of a sign."

CHAPTER TWENTY-THREE

*B*eth's phone was buzzing. Wearily, she opened
her eyes and fumbled for it on her bedside table.

It wasn't there, but it was still buzzing. Feeling a little
frantic, she started to search under her pillows and beneath
the quilt. But she still couldn't find it.

She'd stayed up until midnight so she could try and call
Blake, but again and again she'd gone straight to his voicemail and, eventually, at two a.m. she'd given up.

She couldn't miss his call. She just couldn't.

The phone stopped and Beth angrily got out of bed and
started pulling off the bed sheets, looking underneath it and
all around it.

But then Mum was at her door, knocking. "Beth! Beth!"
She ran in, waving the home-phone.

"Is it Blake?" Beth dashed forwards, but then realised
there was no way Blake would know her landline number.

Mum was holding the phone in her right hand and gesticulating wildly with her left. She was mouthing something but Beth couldn't work out what it was and, eventually, her mother simply shoved the phone at her and forced her to press it to her ear.

"Hello? Beth?"

"Yes." Beth recognised the voice. "Emily?"

"I'm so glad I got hold of you. I tried your cell but there was no answer."

Beth started pacing up and down, unable to keep still. "Sorry, I heard it ring but I couldn't find it."

"Oh, don't say sorry. It's no matter. But I do have some very important news."

Beth looked up at her mother, who was practically jigging from foot to foot, wide-eyed, trying to read Beth's expression. "News?" Beth's throat tightened.

"We have the results of the competition. I'm sorry it took us so long to get in touch. As you know, we analysed engagement on both yours and Blake's posts. And, well, it was amazing really, there was barely a percentage difference between you."

"Really?" Beth had been certain that Blake's numbers would blow hers out of the water.

"Really. It was incredibly close. So close that the judges had quite a tough time choosing a winner."

Beth sucked air past her teeth and puffed out her chest, bracing herself for the blow she knew was coming, the words she'd anticipated ever since she'd found out that Blake was the other finalist. *Thank you for taking part, you came second.*

"Beth?"

"Yes?"

"You're our winner."

For a long time, Beth and her mum squealed, jumped up and down, waved their arms in the air, and cried. In the midst of it all, Emily said she'd email more details and Beth flung the phone onto the bed triumphantly.

Finally, out of breath and trembling with adrenaline, Beth sank down on the floor beside her dressing table and shook her head. "I can't believe it, Mum. I did it."

Her mother sat down beside her and wrapped an arm around her daughter's shoulders. "I knew you would."

Then, slowly, the fizzing, popping, electric excitement she'd felt when Emily said the word 'winner' stared to fade. And Beth's stomach tightened into a fierce knot. "This means..."

Mum looked at her and squeezed her knee. "It means you're going to go travelling around the world."

Beth swallowed hard, suddenly picturing her mother all alone, floating from room to room with no one to talk to, just memories of her father. "I can't leave you," she whispered.

"You absolutely *can* Beth Greenwood. In fact, you have to. This is not something you turn down."

Standing up, Beth ran to her laptop, opened her emails and started searching for one from Emily. "It's a ticket for two people. You could come with me," she said, scanning the rules to see if there was some clause that said mothers weren't allowed.

Behind her, Mum got up and placed her hands on Beth's shoulders. "My darling girl, sit down. I've got something to tell you."

Beth's hands started to shake. The last time she'd heard those words, her parents had been telling her that Dad wouldn't come home from the hospital. She turned around and grabbed hold of her mother's hands.

Mum breathed in deeply and chewed the corner of her bottom lip. "Beth, I..."

"What is it?"

"I met someone." Mum's mouth curled into a soft, hesitant smile.

Beth frowned.

"He works at the hospital with me. He's new. Well, not very new. He's been there a year, but up to now we've just been friends." Mum took out her phone and started swiping through her pictures. "Here, this is him - Greg. He's very nice and, well, I like him. It's early days and it might not go anywhere and I'm still full of so many mixed up feelings about your father, but he's made me realise that I can still have a life."

"So, you're saying you can't come with me because you want to stay with Greg?" Beth had thought about her mum meeting someone new, and how she'd feel about it. She'd always thought she would be angry, or upset, but now that it was happening she just felt confused.

"No, sweetheart. I'm saying I can't come with you because this is *your* journey. I'm telling you about Greg because I want you to see that I'm doing okay. I'm not the same person I was – losing your father changed me. And it changed you too. So, maybe it's time the two of us both learned a bit more about ourselves. Our new selves."

"Can't we learn together?" Beth swiped at her cheeks, which were already slick with tears.

Mum smiled. "Of course we can. We can Skype and email, we can write postcards, maybe I can even come visit you at one of your stops. Bali. Or the Maldives." Mum laughed and kissed Beth's forehead. "But I think you and I both know who you need to take with you on this trip. It's just a question of whether you're brave enough to ask him..."

CHAPTER TWENTY-FOUR

THREE WEEKS LATER

*E*mily had arranged for them to meet at a trendy coffee shop in Central Toronto. Beth spotted her instantly - slick hair, bottle-green blazer, notepad in front of her and a cameraman beside her. She looked up and waved, beckoning Beth towards her.

Beth's stomach tightened. Opposite Emily, in his characteristic checked shirt, Blake was nursing a large cappuccino and tapping his foot against the hard-wood floor. He turned his head. And as soon as he saw her, his eyes widened. He started to get up, then lingered awkwardly above his seat, looking from Beth to Emily and back to Beth as if he might be hallucinating.

Beth straightened her sweater, suddenly wishing she'd

chosen something more glamourous. But finally, Blake stood up and walked towards her.

The cameraman shifted a little and Beth self-consciously tucked a strand of hair behind her ear.

"Beth? They didn't say you were..." Blake straightened his shoulders and glanced at the camera, smiling. "They said it was the loser's interview."

"I'm afraid I asked them to say that. I wanted to surprise you." They were standing no more than a foot apart but Beth could feel the warmth of his body vibrating towards her. She wanted to slip her hands into his, tuck herself under his chin, wrap her arms around him and breathe him in. Her voice was shaky. The freckles of green in his eyes were making her feel wobbly. And, all of a sudden, she felt horribly sure she was about to make a fool of herself.

Behind Blake, Emily nodded and mouthed, *Go on...*

Blake moved a little closer and lowered his voice. All around them, people were starting to shush one another, aware something significant was happening. "What are you doing here, Beth?"

"I won the competition."

Blake laughed a little and his mouth spread into an ironic grin. "Well, yeah, I know. But there really was no need to come all the way to Canada and gloat... you could have sent an email."

"I'm not here to gloat."

Blake blinked at her, slowly. She could tell he was trying

to keep up appearances - show everyone he was confident and unfazed. But his eyes softened as he looked at her in a way that told her he was shaking on the inside.

Beth took a deep breath. "I got your postcards."

Blake's eyes darted to the pendant that hung around her neck. With one finger, he reached out and stroked it. "I see that."

"How in the world did you find it?"

"I thought I was crazy, to be honest." Blake smiled, shaking his head at himself. "I rode the Maiden of the Mist every day for three days and then I spotted it. I thought I was imagining things. It was just sitting there, right on the corner of these rocks."

"And you went down there and got it?"

He shrugged, as if it was nothing.

Lowering her voice, Beth inched closer, meeting his eyes and taking in those heavenly flecks of green. "Why didn't you tell me how you felt?"

Gently, Blake stroked the side of her face. "Because I was a fool?"

"I was waiting... The whole time you were writing those postcards, I was waiting for you to say something. To tell me that we were more than just friends."

"You were?" Blake's eyes looked moist and he swiped at them with the back of his hand.

Beth nodded. "But I've had enough of waiting. So..." she inhaled slowly and slid her hands into Blake's. "So, I'm here to tell you that I love you. Insane, fairy-tale, makes you go breaking the law to retrieve lost jewellery kind of love. And I want you to come with me."

Blake blinked slowly, as if he couldn't believe what was happening and might wake-up at any moment. Beneath its shield of scruffy stubble, his jaw twitched. "Come with you?"

"I spoke to Nomad." She moved closer. Blake was stroking the inside of her palms with his forefingers and it was making it hard to concentrate. "When they told me I was the winner, they said it had been a really tough decision. So, I suggested that maybe you and I could share the prize."

Blake looked at Emily, who nodded enthusiastically. "You want us to go around the world *together*?"

"I really, really do... there are some conditions though." She smiled playfully up at him.

"Conditions?"

"We'd have to travel together. The entire year. Just like we did across Canada. Always together. For twelve whole months..."

"I think I can do that." Blake slipped his hand around to the small of her back and pulled her towards him.

"We'd have to combine our blogs - start a new one - write together."

"Done." He brushed her hair from her cheek.

"And we'd have to seal the deal with a kiss..."

Blake smiled, and his Hollywood dimples made her feel weak at the knees. "I can *absolutely* do that one," he whispered. And then, at last, he brushed his lips against hers and they melted into a kiss that made them feel as if they were the only two people in the room.

EPILOGUE

ONE YEAR LATER

"*L*ast stop, London." Blake leaned over and kissed Beth on the cheek. She grinned and scratched playfully at his stubble.

"Do you think when we're not moving country every few weeks, you'll shave a little more often?"

"I thought you liked it." Blake rubbed at his chin. "It's rugged and manly."

"It's prickly. And it gets in the way of me kissing my husband."

Blake turned his back to the aeroplane window and tilted his head at her. "Well, in that case... I guess I should do what my wife tells me to, shouldn't I?"

Beth grinned. "You know what they say... happy wife, happy life!"

"Are you?" Blake suddenly looked serious. He reached for her hand. "Are you happy?"

Beth smiled and squeezed his fingers in hers. "Blake O'Brien, this has been the best year of my life. And don't you ever doubt it."

"Mine too."

"I love you, Mr O'Brien."

"I love you too."

Beth sat up and flipped open her iPad. "But, tell me, as you've decided to do what your wife says, does that mean I'm allowed to pick our next trip?"

"We haven't even finished this one yet!"

"I know. But, look, I saw an article about this tiny little island off the coast of New Zealand... hardly anyone has ever been there, you have to take like three planes and a boat, but it has the most incredible caves, and these huge sparkling lakes, and waterfalls..."

Blake glanced at the screen, skimming over the article and the pictures. "Well," he said, smiling at her. "When we got married, I promised that I'd go to the ends of the Earth for you... so I guess I can't say no, can I?"

THE END

Thank you for reading *Love in the Rockies*.

If you love sweet romance stories with a hint of adventure and a happy ever after, you'll love the other books in the **True Love Travels** *series. All books are available in Kindle Unlimited, and you can grab* **Love in the Alps** *totally free if you sign up to my mailing list at www.poppypennington.com.*

Love in the Rockies

Love in Provence

Love in Tuscany

Love in The Highlands

Love at Christmas

Love in the Alps – Subscriber Exclusive

The first book in my brand news series *A Heart Full of Secrets* will be available in November 2020.

THANK YOU!

Thank you so much for reading *Love in the Rockies*. It's hard for me to say just how much I appreciate my readers. Especially those who get in touch. Please always feel free to email me at poppy@poppypennington.com.

If you enjoyed this book, please consider taking a moment to leave a review on Amazon. Reviews are crucial for an author's success and I would really, sincerely appreciate it.

You can leave a review at:

amazon.com/author/poppypenningtonsmith

goodreads.com/Poppy_Pennington_Smith

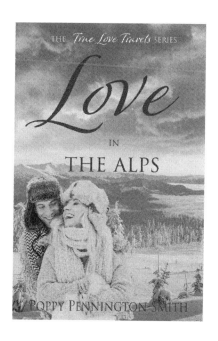

Join Poppy's mailing list to stay up to date with all of her latest releases and download the novelette *Love in the Alps* totally free!

Download Love in the Alps here:
https://dl.bookfunnel.com/boluyc3qig
or visit poppypennington.com

ABOUT POPPY

Poppy Pennington-Smith writes sweet, wholesome romance novels featuring tenacious women and the gorgeous guys who fall for them.

Poppy has always been a romantic at heart. A sucker for a happy ending, she loves writing books that give you a warm, fuzzy feeling.

When she's not running around after Mr. P and Mini P, Poppy can be found drinking coffee from a Frida Kahlo mug, cuddled up in a mustard yellow blanket, and watching the garden from her writing shed.

Poppy's dream-come-true is talking to readers who enjoy her books. So, please do let her know what you think of them.

You can email poppy@poppypennington.com or join the PoppyPennReaders group on Facebook to get in touch.

You can also visit www.poppypennington.com.

Printed in Great Britain
by Amazon